"*Renee!*"

He could make out ... blur moved behind her. L... run. Tyler aimed the gun at ... into his lungs, and then pulled the trigger. The animal growled and kept moving. He shot again, and then again. Rage-filled roars filled the air, and the dark mass fell and remained still.

Tyler stabbed through the dark to find Renee's figure. He saw nothing. "Renee?"

"Here." Her voice trembled. "I'm here."

Teddy bounded out of the darkness. Tyler whistled and the dog took off. Tyler's limbs shook with the shock of the ordeal. He found Renee on the ground, head in her hands. He heard the deep sobs that wrenched through her and knelt beside her. "Hey." She shuddered a breath. "I forgot to tell you to take the rifle."

She didn't answer, the sobs clawing out of her. He touched her shoulder, and she raised her head. He wasn't sure who moved first, but she was in his arms then, her back shuddering beneath his hand.

As they sat there the sheep returned. Slow, spooked, more bunched than normal. But his presence seemed to soothe them and they began to spread out again. And still he held the fragile form in his arms, unable to let go though her tears were spent, her terror diminished.

S. DIONNE MOORE is a multi-published author who makes her home in Pennsylvania with her husband of twenty-one years and her daughter. You can visit her at www.sdionnemoore.com.

Books by S. Dionne Moore

HEARTSONG PRESENTS

HP912—Promise of Tomorrow
HP932—Promise of Yesterday
HP948—Promise of Time

A Shepherd's Song

S. Dionne Moore

Heartsong Presents

To Renee, for paving the way of arthritis, menopause, wrinkles, and bodily malfunctions for your MUCH YOUNGER sister. Still love me? And to Sharon, thanks for being there for mom. I'm so glad we've united. Finally. Love you both!

A note from the Author:
I love to hear from my readers! You may correspond with me by writing:

S. Dionne Moore
Author Relations
PO Box 721
Uhrichsville, OH 44683

ISBN 978-1-61626-540-3

A SHEPHERD'S SONG

All scripture quotations are taken from the King James Version of the Bible.

Our mission is to publish and distribute inspirational products offering exceptional value and biblical encouragement to the masses.

PRINTED IN THE U.S.A.

one

Renee Dover lifted her head to peer over the rock she hid behind. Excitement pumped through her when she saw the four men sprawled out on the ground in various stages of rest. Only one of the four showed signs of wakefulness, his attention glued to the stick he whittled. A small pile of shavings covered his lap and peppered the ground around his thighs.

The easy motion of the knife against the wood worked another curl from the stick. He lowered the knife and raised his head. Renee ducked behind her rock, her initial thrill oozing into an uneasy feeling that snaked through her veins. All at once, she recognized the foolhardiness that had led her to bait her brother into the hills to try to find the hideout of the Loust Gang. Now that she had stumbled upon their camp, the knowledge that her brother was in the hills on the other side of the valley reinforced the fact that she was alone. With four outlaws. And a gun she had shot only three times before.

Stories of the Loust Gang's deeds swelled in her memory. Her pa worried that their ranch was too close to the Loust Gang's new territory and might be visited by the outlaws, prompting in Renee all types of romantic notions about finding the gang and collecting the reward. And now here she crouched, looking right at them. A shudder trickled through her as she slowly backed away from the rock.

"Renee?"

She inhaled sharply at the sound of her brother's voice, distant, calling from the valley floor. She glanced back toward the men to see if they'd heard Thomas's call. The man with the stick lifted his head. Renee ducked down and shifted to the right where a large, prickly bush with no leaves allowed her to see the men but shielded her from view. The lanky man's eyes probed the area where Renee hid. He stared for a long minute, bent one knee, propped his arm along it, and continued to whittle.

"Renee? Shoot your gun so I know where you are."

Thomas's voice was closer. Louder. Renee squeezed her eyes shut. If she didn't answer, he would continue up the hill and get caught. She had to warn him away, but how could she without risking her own safety?

The lanky man rose to his feet this time. He buckled on his guns and toed the man next to him. "Rand, get up. Someone's coming," he hissed.

"Let Lance take care of them," the portly man mumbled before releasing a yawn.

The slender man kicked the man harder. "Get up. I don't know where Lance is. He shouldn't have let anyone wander this close."

"Maybe he fell asleep," Rand mumbled as he frowned up at the skinny man. "With you hollerin', he'll wake up and take care of things. Stop your worrying."

"Renee!"

Thomas's voice rang clearer, closer than before. The tall man's head jerked and his eyes narrowed. Renee's heart slammed. Even Rand lifted his head then elbowed himself to a sitting position.

The slender man's head rotated one way, then the other, eyes scanning, before he started in the direction from which Thomas's voice had come. He drew closer to Renee, so near that if she so much as twitched, he would notice. Her heart thundered now, ears roaring with the fear that swelled in her throat. His hand hovered over his right gun. Behind him, Rand marched to the other two outlaws and barked at them to get up and buckle on their guns.

Renee huddled into a tighter ball, afraid to move and afraid not to. She closed her eyes and strained for the sound of Thomas's horse. If they spotted him, she would jump up and hopefully divert their attention while Thomas used his six-shooters. He'd been practicing with his new guns and was good. Much better than she. But if the outlaws got off a shot first. . .

She held her breath and waited.

"Ya seen Lance?" Rand's voice whispered, close at hand.

"Guard the gold," the slender man growled back. "Tell Lolly to keep watch to the west, and Dirk to the east."

Sweat trickled down Renee's back, her ears primed for any hint that the slender man had spotted someone and was going to draw. She could see his cruel face in her mind's eye, and she had no doubt whatsoever that he knew how to use those six-shooters on his hips. She exhaled long and slow, haunted by the memory of the article in the latest edition of the town newspaper, already two weeks old when her pa had brought it home, that reported the latest body count as a result of the Loust Gang's thievin' ways was six.

A shot rang out, and Renee gasped and jerked her head up.

"Got 'em, boss!" a deep voice barked up the hill. A new voice.

Thomas! Renee's stomach rolled. Her fault. All her fault. The distant sound of a galloping horse came to her ears then disappeared. Probably Thomas's horse, riderless, returning to the ranch. Pa would be devastated. Her throat burned and tears collected in her eyes. Her body tensed.

"Thought you'd fallen asleep on us," the lanky man said, his hands relaxed at his sides now. She could see the cruelty of his mouth. He scratched along his jaw, his eyes sweeping the rock-littered hillside.

A horse whinnied, and the clop of hooves alerted her to the movements of another man, probably the Lance Rand had mentioned. She would be trapped. And it didn't matter. Not with Thomas dead. She deserved to die, too. Renee slid out from the bush, her back to the camp, her legs stiff from the hunched position.

She heard quick footsteps behind her, just as a horse trotted up the hill into view. Two more seconds and the man on the horse would see her. She didn't care. She stood and faced the lanky fellow just as the horseman hollered out from behind her.

"Boss!"

The lanky fellow's head whipped her direction and a gun appeared in his hand, the cold eye of the barrel pointed at her chest. "Get over here where I can see you. You have a gun; shuck it now."

She grabbed the lone gun in the holster awkwardly buckled around her hips. For the journey into the hills, she'd begged Thomas to let her wear a pair of his pants.

Lanky's jaw clenched, though she thought she saw amusement in his eyes. "Got ourselves a boy." His eyes raked down her. "Correction. A girl playing like a boy."

At her back, the clop of hooves stopped and she heard a sardonic laugh. "Prettiest boy I ever seen. What you going to do with her, boss?"

A low whistle rent the air, and Renee followed the movement of Rand and the other outlaws coming toward her. She didn't know which had whistled.

"Fine catch, Marv," Rand said. "Mighty fine."

The lanky man didn't move. She felt his gaze on her but kept her eyes averted, chin high. She would not cry.

"You must be Renee," he finally said.

She refused to look at him and stared, instead, at the horizon, where the sun's color touched the bellies of the clouds, turning them pink. She heard the crunch of his footfall and the blur of motion before a painful vise clamped her arm.

"Look at me when I talk to you," he snarled.

Renee gasped as pain shot up her arm. She faced him, beating down the fear that worse treatment was to come, even as anger flushed through her. "Leave me alone."

A smile shot across his face and he let her go. "Anything you wish, m'lady. Shall I have a noble knight show you to your chambers?"

The men bunched in closer, sharing a good laugh over their leader's wit. Her breathing quickened and her scalp tingled. She did the only thing she knew to show her disgust. She spat, just like Thomas had shown her, and the nasty wad landed right on Marv's shirt.

Silence fell over the group as Marv stared down at his shirt then back at her. His eyes flashed cold and she tensed, waiting for his wrath to fall. But he only stared, muscles trembling along his jaw.

"Well?" she said, her voice sharp, unable to stand his silence a moment longer. "Aren't you going to shoot me?"

"I don't pull lead on a lady." His eyes narrowed and a smirk curled his lips. "Unless I'm provoked or there's something in it for me..." He lifted a hand. "Rand!"

The potbellied man stepped forward, eagerness to please evident in his demeanor.

"Take the *lady*"—he drawled the word—"to the cave and stay there with her until I decide what to do with her. Do whatever you need to keep her under control." He pivoted and took two steps, his head whipping side to side. "Lance, get back on watch. Lolly, Dirk, pack things up. We're moving down toward the valley."

two

Tyler Sperry patted the grungy, smelly hound and pushed the rabbit he'd just shot closer to the dog. The hound didn't hesitate, his floppy ears waving, mere ribbons from the many fights he'd had with the coyotes and the snakes. Alerted by the hound's return to camp, Tyler's sheepdog, Teddy, woke and began to move, goading the sheep to their feet. Tyler loved the rhythm of the two dogs. The hound hunted and kept predators at bay, seldom coming into camp, and Teddy worked the sheep daily, ferreting out those that had wandered during the night and moving them when needed. Exactly what Tyler was needing now as he led the herd into the mountains where it would be cooler in the summer months.

Tired, Tyler shuffled to his horse. He stooped and ran his hands down the horse's legs and over her hocks, feeling for the telltale warmth that spoke of pulled tendons. The horse shifted her weight and craned her neck to playfully nip at Tyler's shoulder. "On with you now, Sassy." But the horse's playfulness brought a smile to his lips. He stood and brushed his hand down the horse's back. "You take a swipe at me again and I just might leave you to the bandits. They'd like a horse like you."

Indeed, few cowhands possessed long-legged, powerful horses like Sassy. He'd thought of selling the animal for a smaller horse when he took the job as sheepherder, but he chose to keep her because of the history between them. He ran a finger over the scar on her right shoulder, and his lower knee ached at the reminder of the bullet that had grazed the horse and lodged in his leg.

Tyler saddled his horse and walked Sassy around the camp. "Go ahead and let it out, girl. You know I'm going to cinch you up tighter."

Sassy nickered, and Tyler stooped to tighten the cinch strap where the horse had finally let out her breath. "Can't play the same trick day in and day out and not expect me to catch on." He grinned as he mounted and picked up the reins. *But you do try.*

Lifting his head, he gave a low whistle, and Teddy appeared from the bunched flock. He nodded in satisfaction. "Good boy, Teddy. Go easy on them, now."

Tyler twisted in his saddle and kept a sharp look as Teddy zigzagged behind the sheep, always keeping them moving forward with quiet efficiency, though the young lambs challenged Teddy's efforts. Satisfied that Teddy was working well, Tyler led the herd toward the taller grasses where the sheep would spend much of the morning munching and drinking water from the streams.

As they approached the verdant hillside, the sheep spread out. The old hound trailed Teddy by a few hundred yards. Tyler knew the dog's instincts would drive him to disappear among the trees and hills that surrounded the herd to look for signs of predators. He cast his eyes over the herd, satisfied to see Teddy setting an invisible boundary where he patrolled the sheep to prevent them from escaping on the side opposite the stream.

Tyler dismounted and climbed onto a boulder to survey the sheep, especially the three pregnant ewes. The other mamas had delivered, but these three were late. He kept his eyes on the herd but allowed his mind to wander. The sunshine warmed him and deepened his weariness. Tomorrow he would need to break camp and move the sheep farther uphill, a good four miles.

As always, the silence both soothed him and made him restless. He loved the peace of the sheepherder's life and hated the isolation. Yet it was the path he had chosen. Had been forced to choose. And he had only himself to blame.

A distant bark brought his mind back to the sheep. Most of the flock went about their grazing, not spooked by the sound, though Tyler knew if the dog continued, the sheep would begin to react. Before he could move to investigate, the hound appeared on a rock ledge above the herd, tongue lolling to one side.

The animal usually howled at coyotes, gaining enough of a response from the predators to enable him to find their location. This was different, though. Tyler climbed off the rock, his palm scraping when his foot slid. He took a moment to remove a leather sack from the pack behind Sassy's saddle. From the pack he took out a piece of thin linen and awkwardly wrapped it around his palm to stop the bleeding. He pulled his rifle from the scabbard and set out.

❧

Every nerve in Renee's body tightened. The stone bit into her back as she shifted to try to see where Rand had wandered off to. Since their arrival at the new location three days ago, he had hardly said two words to her, not that she minded. His rotten teeth repelled her, and the oily glances he sent her way stirred fear in her stomach.

Though he had not tied her, she could see that he was a man—that they were all men—who would let their guns rule any situation. Rand would not be sweet-talked, and she would be crazy not to try to escape. Long into the night she had considered and dismissed several options. Rand stuck close to her. She would have to be careful.

On quiet feet, she moved to the mouth of the shallow cave that had become her new home and peeked out. Rand stood some distance off, his arms loose at his sides, his gaze on some point distant, as if he was listening to something. Or for someone. Was Rand expecting Marv and the rest of the gang? The dawning of opportunity stacked tension along her spine, but the sight of Rand's guns gave her pause.

She owed it to her pa to at least try. Better for him to find out about Thomas than to agonize when neither of his children returned. Even now, she knew he must be sick with fear, if only for Thomas. She doubted he would grieve much over her disappearance.

Renee closed her eyes. She blew a frustrated breath and continued her study of the area. She had to focus on her mission. As they had traveled, she'd tried to keep track of the direction they'd gone, but the constant switching back had left her confused. Regardless, she would escape first and then worry about getting home.

A bush rustled beside the cave entrance where she stood. She tensed for the appearance of a snake, but the blur within the branches seemed larger. A brown mottled face poked out of the brush. A dog.

Stunned, Renee could only stare at the animal. Where had he come from? When he emerged, she saw his shredded ears and the scars along his face and shoulders where hair did not grow. The dog sat down, gave one short bark, then turned tail and scampered back through the brush and emerged as a black blur on the other side.

"That stupid dog." Rand's footsteps closed her window of opportunity. She wanted to hate the dog for his bark, but at the sight of the sorrowful mess of his ears and face, sympathy stabbed through her. The poor mongrel was probably skulking about looking for food.

"Mutt came sniffing around the other night, too. Heard a coyote in the distance and it took off running. Probably scared silly."

Renee doubted it. Maybe the dog was hunting coyotes and smelled them in the form of Rand, Marv, and all his cohorts. The thought plucked the first smile she'd enjoyed since being captured. It slid from her lips, though, when she recalled all that had happened and the way Marv had looked at her that first night after her capture. She shuddered. If she couldn't escape first, she would have to fight hard against their lecherous attempts in hopes they would shoot her dead.

With nothing left to do, she went deep into the cave and lay down. She didn't know how long she slept, but when she woke the sun had dipped farther toward the west. Rand remained in the same place, dozing by the looks of things, but she didn't want to get too close, realizing that his inattention afforded her an opportunity.

She surveyed the area around her again. Purple lupine contrasted the yellow orange of the poppies to create a riot of color. Such a contrast to the ugliness of the situation she now faced. Other than a few scrubby bushes, the lupine and the curved branches of the prickly cactus, she had no other coverage on the hillside. Rand's guns would find her long before she put enough distance between them to feel safe.

Renee turned to stare down the back of the cave—the same direction the dog had taken earlier. Her heart slammed hard and perspiration beaded along her back as she considered the more densely populated side of the hill. Time was of the essence, for she knew that Rand could come alert at any moment and realize his mistake in not keeping a closer eye on her. From where he sat, the cave would cover her disappearance for a few minutes at most.

With a steadying breath, Renee ducked beneath the thick bush and followed a strange, low arch formed in the branches, as if wild animals knew of the tunnel of brush and traipsed through it often. She debated staying there, hidden from view, but just as quickly realized the folly of simply hiding when she had the chance to put more distance between herself and her captor. Branches snarled her hair and tore at her clothing as she pushed forward. She gasped at the pinches of pain from the poking branches and squinted her eyes to protect them against damage. When the sunlight brightened, she realized the branch cover was thinning. She paused for a moment at the end of the arching tunnel to collect herself for the run down the rest of the hillside and said a prayer, out of desperation more than faith, that she wouldn't feel a bullet in her back. That the Lord might, just this once, give her the desires of her heart.

three

Tyler followed the hound from a distance. He had no doubt that the animal's instincts had picked up on something out of the ordinary, but he also wasn't fool enough to stick too close to the animal should the problem be bigger than one man could handle. He knew outlaws used the mountains and valleys as cover, places to elude capture, and he had no desire to walk into a hill of fire ants such as that. Shutting the mouths of anyone who would discover their whereabouts would be their first reaction, and the rocky ground and spring flowers would mark the site of his final resting place.

The dog halted and crouched. Tyler stopped as well, sighting up the hills on either side of him for any signs of wildlife, either the outlaw variety or the four-legged kind. Seeing nothing, he glanced back at the crouched dog just as the hound lunged forward and snapped his teeth. Tyler understood at once what the dog was doing. The long, limp body in the hound's jaws didn't surprise him at all. Long ago, he had learned of the animal's prowess at killing rattlers, though he'd also almost lost that battle a number of times.

When the dog spit out the body and gave it a sniff as if to assure himself of the serpent's death, he moved forward. At one point, he paused and glanced over his powerful shoulder, and Tyler knew the animal was making sure he was still keeping up. Interest piqued by the hound's behavior, Tyler picked up his pace to close the distance between them.

He skirted a large boulder, his eyes roaming the landscape, when he became aware that the hound had stopped. Tyler's eyes narrowed as he scanned up the hill. He immediately picked up on movement and raised his gun. His quick assessment determined the target to be a woman. He followed her path down the hill. The hound stood at his side, hackles raised, though he remained quiet.

Tyler flung himself behind the rock and readjusted his aim, his finger on the trigger, tense but loose. The woman kept coming. She lost her footing on the rocks and skidded, catching herself and pushing upward again. And that's when it came.

A shot rang out and the woman went down, whether from fright or because she was hit, Tyler didn't know. His gaze darted along the ridge of the hill, pinpointing a lone figure. He squinted down the barrel and returned fire, aiming low, his intention to maim rather than kill. The man jerked and disappeared, and Tyler set aside the gun and dashed up the hill to the fallen woman. She lay in a heap not two hundred feet away and began to move just as Tyler dropped down on his knees beside her. Seconds ticked by as he picked her up in his arms, knowing a bullet could crease him, or worse, at any given second.

He skidded to his knees a couple of feet from the boulder, the woman in his arms just beginning to thrash her protest. He released her and snapped up his Sharps, leveling it at the ridge again. He could see nothing. Satisfied, he scanned the woman from head to foot, searching for blood or signs of injury. "You hit?"

Her stormy eyes sparked of fear more than the bravado her crouched position and clawed hands threatened. Her chest heaved with the rapidness of her breaths. Tyler had seen that look more times than he wanted to count. It was the stance taken not by the hunters, but by the hunted.

❧

Unshed tears of panic filled Renee's eyes. She tried to slow the quickened slam of her heart and ease the rush of fear as the strange man picked up his gun and fired. He had asked her something, but the words were lost to her in the cloud of gun smoke and fear as she waited for the moment when he would turn the gun on her. Truth fought to insert itself in her mind. Why would a man shoot at her after carrying her down the hill and away from danger?

He straightened, glancing her way. "I'll take the fact you're still on your feet as a no."

Moisture bunched in her eyes, and she blinked to clear her vision.

He picked up the rifle and she flinched, wondering what such a long-reaching gun would do to her at close range. She stiffened and opened her mouth. He never raised the gun, instead holding it out to her.

"I'm going up the hill. Cover me."

She wanted to tell him not to, that Rand waited up there, but the words knotted in her throat. He moved out fast and scampered up the hill even faster. A dog ran at his side and some vague familiarity scratched at her mind as she watched the tattered ears flop with every step.

The man slipped on the steep slope but caught himself, his hand catching in a nearby cactus. She winced for him. When he righted himself, he kept low to the ground. Renee raised her gaze to the place where she'd emerged, afraid Rand would appear at any moment, his gun aimed at the stranger.

She stretched against the rock and lifted the weapon to her eye. She was no perfect shot, but maybe she could dampen Rand's desire to nail her rescuer. Grateful for the steadying effect the boulder offered to her shaking hands, she continued to follow the line of the man's advance up the hill. When he reached the ridge, he disappeared over the crest. She waited in silent expectation. Horror swelled as minutes passed and he didn't reappear. Only the fact that she heard no gunfire kept her from giving in to her nerves. If Marv had heard the two gunshots, he would rush to the cave. The stranger would be ambushed. Killed. She would be alone again.

She kept her eyes hard on the place where the blue of the sky met the curve of the hilltop. She debated making a run for it. Here she was, again, hiding from the Loust Gang when an opportunity to flee was open to her. But she couldn't leave the stranger. He had rescued her. He counted on her. Just as Pa had counted on her to stop her wild ways and become a lily-skinned do-gooder—a daughter he could be proud of.

Renee lifted her head and relaxed her hold on the rifle. If the stranger got caught, he at least had the hound. If she got caught, she had the gun. But she was more vulnerable to a gang of men than he was. They would hang him or shoot him dead, but they'd do far worse to her before finally putting a bullet into her heart. She couldn't think about it. Wouldn't. Instead she leaned forward against the rock. She would give him some time.

He would return.

He had to.

four

Tyler scanned the area at the top of the hill from right to left. A small fire struggled for lack of new fuel. He shifted his gaze to the hound that stood a few feet off staring at the empty campsite, frozen by duty, muscles tensed to bring down any enemy sighted. Only a soft breeze ruffled his fur. Tyler knew the animal's senses were keen, probably much sharper than his own, so when the animal finally turned and trotted back down the hill, Tyler knew whoever had shot at the girl had disappeared.

He took his time gathering what little information he could from the signs left behind. Footprints circled the campfire. Boots. Narrow toes and deep heel marks gave clue to the man's weight. He found, too, the place behind the boulder where the man had sprawled, the outline of his body deeper in the middle where his belly lay. Tyler also made note of the depressions where the man propped himself before raising to the rock. On the right, the blur wasn't as deep and the indentation larger. Right handed. He had shifted weight to his left elbow to settle the gun or check the load.

Armed with enough information about the girl's enemy, Tyler tried to make sense of it all. Outlaws? He'd not heard of a group hiding out in these mountains since rumors of Big Nose George and Frank Cassidy. He raised his hat to wipe the sweat from his forehead as a sickening burn lanced his stomach. Could be nothing more than a lonesome band of drifters up to no good.

Tyler picked up a stick and used it to scatter the fire, waiting for the flames to dwindle, then kicked dirt on the remaining embers until the smoke dissipated. With one last sweeping glance, he took in the vacant area before starting down the hill. He wondered if the girl had taken off back toward her home, or if she'd waited for him as he'd suggested.

His foot skidded. His right hand skimmed the ground. Fire stabbed his already-raw palm as the rocks and gravel bit deep. He winced and pushed himself upright, swiping his hands against the rough wool of his trousers. His breath caught as the raw wound burned. He glanced behind him at the hills that gave way to the Big Horns as his palm cooled, then to the relatively flat land spread out west and north of where he stood. In the distance he could see the hound, already on its way back to its duties. He marveled at the animal's instinct and loyalty. With more cautious steps, Tyler continued down, pressed by the idea of the man returning to the camp, bent on vengeance.

As Tyler neared the bottom, the young woman's head popped up from behind the boulder, her eyes huge. She held out the gun to him, and he noticed the tremor in her hand and the vacant glaze of her eyes. She was going to cry by the looks of it.

Tyler took the gun and broke it to check the load and to avoid watching the girl's distress. Probably a reaction from what she'd just endured. He'd seen it all before, but it never ceased to churn nausea in his stomach.

"I'm Renee. Dover's my last name."

Her voice trembled, but a hard note showed the determination with which she tried to hold on to her composure. Tyler snapped the gun shut and shoved it into the scabbard. Now that he'd done his duty by her. . . What now? He had to return to his flock, and he doubted very seriously she would be placated at the idea of going with him.

Bracing his arm against the saddle, he leaned against Sassy's warm side and stroked her neck. "You live 'round here?"

"I did."

Something in her tone made him straighten and pay attention. She turned her back to him and walked a few paces, hugging herself. Her head dipped, and quiet sobs grated against his need to put distance between them.

He stared up at Sassy as if the horse could offer a solution to his dilemma then took up the reins and mounted. "Needing to get back, ma'am."

She spun with a gasp. "You can't leave me here."

Of course he couldn't. But neither could he bring himself to offer to take her along. Wasn't right for a single man to be gallivanting with a single woman. Especially a woman like her.

❧

Across the distance, Renee saw his gaze dip to his hands resting on the pommel. She didn't care how it might look; he couldn't leave her here. Alone. With only her burning anger to keep her warm, no food and no horse. Renee didn't want to beg but she would if she had to. Surely he could see her problem and understand the precariousness of her position.

"I've got a flock of sheep to tend. You'll have to stay in camp as I move them." He lifted his gaze to hers. "With me. Alone."

Were his words a challenge? If the man rescued her, surely it meant he had a healthy sense of honor.

"Your. . .flock?"

"I'm a shepherd. A sheepherder."

She never would have guessed it by his looks, but then, what could one really discern by something so deceiving? Her pa had mentioned a rancher taking on sheep over by Sheridan. It had been a vague comment made many months ago, and she remembered little else other than her father's contempt for any man trying to run anything other than cattle.

Renee wished she could see the man's eyes, but they were shadowed by the brim of his hat. His angular jaw and the bristle of beard gave him a hard appearance, not unlike the men he'd just rescued her from. But a gentle face did not a gentleman make, although the reverse was also true. That much she knew.

Still, what choice did she have? She wished mightily that she had not surrendered the rifle to him—or that she still had her own weapon. The man swung the horse away. A chill swept over her at the thought of being alone. She stepped closer to him and reached a hand to stroke the horse's nose. The animal stretched out her neck and nibbled Renee's sleeve.

"I can walk," she offered, not wanting to give overtaxing the horse as more reason for him to leave her behind.

The man didn't argue and gave the horse a soft jab. Open mouthed at his quick dismissal of her, and his failure to even offer her a chance to ride, she could only watch as the horse put distance between them.

five

Surely she didn't expect to be treated like a lady. What woman would wear pants and then expect preferential treatment? He still believed a woman should look like a woman and not gallivant around in trousers or buckskins or anything other than a dress. Besides, it was her idea to walk. Still, the dusty memory of gentlemanly ways and manners taught to him by his mama made him purse his lips and frown. He fought the silent battle for about half a mile, haunted by images of what the man might have done to her. The horrors she might have endured. It was the mental picture of his mother's disapproving frown that goaded him. With a sigh that was more a moan, he stopped the horse and slid to the ground. "You ride."

"I can walk."

A burst of quick, hot anger shot through him. "Get on the horse." Her horrified expression made him bite back the flash of his temper. He should know better than to speak so roughly. She was, no doubt, tired, and by the way she dressed, a bit willful. Commanding her to do anything would not hasten his return to his flock. "Please," he added. "That man can still follow our trail. It's best we move fast."

"Men."

He could only stare at her.

"There was four of them, maybe five. They'll kill us."

"Best get to it, then." He patted the saddle.

"Shouldn't you ride as well?"

Deciding to seize the moment, he heaved a sigh and toed his boot into the stirrup, sweeping back into the saddle. He kicked his foot out and reached out his hand to offer aid in her ascent. She grasped his hand and hauled herself up. For the first time he realized what a gift it was that she did not wear skirts. The saddle was crowded enough with her presence. When she placed a tentative hand at his waist as he wheeled the horse, the shift in wind direction brought a light, sweet scent to his nostrils. He frowned, the smell mocking somehow, evidence of what he'd missed by not settling down at a young age with a good girl like his mama had wanted.

Her slender hand gripped his shirt harder when he dug his heels hard into Sassy's sides and took them to a ground-eating gallop. When he figured they'd gone a mile, he stopped, wheeled the horse, and studied the terrain behind him. No signs of dust rising into the air to indicate pursuit. Behind him, Renee remained quiet, yet he was more aware of her presence than he wanted to be every time he caught that sniff of sweetness.

An hour had passed when he relieved Sassy of the wicked pace he'd set and they began the climb up the eastern slope of the mountain. Within an hour the sheep finally came into view. All seemed well, though the sheep had scattered a bit, even under Teddy's watchful eye. He stopped at a boulder. "This is where we stop. We've put a few miles between us. I'm moving the herd up this mountain. It'll take a couple of weeks, maybe more, depending." He did as much as he could to help her dismount smoothly, unsettled by the need to touch her hand, and the feel of her hand brushing his shoulder then gripping his forearms. "Stay here."

He could tell by the stiffening of her spine and her dark frown that she resented his command. Tough. He had a herd to move, and that she got herself into trouble wasn't his fault. He would protect her, even try to get her back home safe, but she'd have to wait. It might be a long wait, too, but if he told her that, she'd probably stomp her foot and pout.

He stole a look at her and wondered how she would feel about staying in a camp with nothing but sheep, nature, two dogs, and a horse to keep her company. No doubt she'd not like it too much. But he'd chosen his path for a reason, and he'd sooner stick to his reasons than leave the herd defenseless and let down Rich Morgan.

In the small camp, he let Sassy drink long from the bucket of water he'd fetched that morning. As the horse drank, he took down his tent. He rolled his coffee, sugar, flour, dry beans, and salt pork into two bundles and stuck them into his saddlebags. His pan, plate, fork, tin cup, and blanket were rolled up in the center of the tent, and the entire bundle covered with oilcloth. The familiarity of the work soothed him and made him forget the girl. At least until he glimpsed her movement along the perimeter of the campsite. When he motioned to her, she started his way. Teddy came to his side, as if sensing the tension. Tyler picked up the last thing left at the campsite, his Bible, and gripped it hard as he prepared for what he knew would be a verbal showdown.

❧

Renee could only think of home. Of Thomas. She wanted, no, *needed*, to go home. She set her jaw and moved forward, directly into the milling sheep that moved away as she drew near. The small dog beside Tyler came alert as she approached. Not unfriendly, but his tail didn't wag either, and she wondered if getting too close might be a bad idea.

"If you're heading higher into the mountains, then it's best to get me home now."

Tyler stared hard at her. "Should have stayed home then and not gotten caught by that band of brigands."

"It wasn't my fault, they—" Her oft-repeated phrase held no conviction. It *was* her fault. Adventure was something she always longed for and never failed to find. Her mouth turned sour at the realization that her wild imaginations had helped to lay Thomas out cold. He hadn't wanted to go, but she'd persisted and gotten her way. Again.

Renee closed her eyes and clenched her fists. Face to face with her hardheaded ways. Thomas's words of caution rang in her ears. He often pleaded on behalf of their silent pa on the matter of her willfulness. Words she often chafed at and always ignored.

Now, when tears of repentance should come, she felt nothing but a dusty, arid emptiness.

six

Tyler's hand sweat against the cover of the Bible as he watched her, captivated by the shifting emotions that at one moment pinched Renee's features then shifted to stark vulnerability. She was a young woman. Alone. And he had been a man alone, too. For too long to deny the appeal of having another person to talk to and interact with, even if only for a few days.

"I can't take you home. Got to stay with the woolies and get them to higher pasture before the hot temperatures get on us."

She blinked at him like a newborn lamb testing the light of the world for the first time.

"You mean you're staying *here*?"

He allowed himself a grin. "Well, no. Not *here*." Her pique was evident in her stormy gaze. He smoothed his hand down Sassy's side and opened the saddlebag to slide the Bible into its little niche. "As I said, I need to move them higher." There was no choice in the matter. Not for him. Not now. He'd already crossed the narrow bend of the path that was one of the most dangerous. If he left the sheep now and they wandered back to the familiar, he'd lose some over that ledge, and he held a stake in this herd. When Rich Morgan sent out his camptender to deliver supplies to Tyler in another couple of months, he could send her back then. Let Rich deal with figuring out how to get the girl home.

"I can't just stay out here. With you—"

He jerked her direction, working to bite back hard words. She would not understand the isolation he was forced to endure. And why would she? She was a young woman wanting to go home after being held by a band of men probably not fit for human society. "That's the way it's got to be, Renee." He tripped over her name. Saying it seemed so strange. A woman, here, in his camp. An event beyond his comprehension.

"If I leave the sheep alone, they will scatter and die. I watch them for a man by the name of Rich Morgan, and I've a stake in the herd, too." He gathered Sassy's reins and led the horse to the boulder. "Need help getting on? Four miles is a long way on foot." She didn't look at all happy with him. She stared around as if trying to figure out the direction she should go. Wide eyes met his, and he felt compelled to apologize. "As soon as someone comes, I'll send you back. But not until then."

She brightened, and he knew she misunderstood the promise inherent in his words.

"That could be two months. Maybe more."

Her expression crumbled. "You can't make me go with you."

"No. Frankly, it's easier if I don't have you with me."

"Then I'll make my own way."

"And risk becoming prey to the mountain lions or those men all over again? Who's to say they aren't looking for you right now?"

Her eyes settled on him. He could see the flecks of gold in the smoky gray expression. Strange eyes. Yet beautiful. He shook himself. No use letting his mind go soft just because he had a woman in camp. He stabbed the pointed toe of his boot into the stirrup and mounted up. When he glanced over his shoulder and raised an eyebrow, she remained rooted to the spot.

"You left them to come get me."

"No. I left them to follow the mutt. You just happened to be part of the bargain." No need to tell her she was only partly right. Following the mutt usually meant finding evidence of coyotes or other predators who might hunt the sheep. When the dog had led him so far out, sheer curiosity had made him follow. He'd begun to wonder if the dog was getting too old for the work when he'd discovered Renee. How he'd wished then he'd yielded to his instinct to break off trailing the mutt. No use fretting on it now, though. What was done was done.

Tyler urged Sassy along, throwing over his shoulder, "Go or stay, it makes no difference to me."

❧

How dare he leave her standing there. He gave a long whistle and the little dog came to life. It skittered out in as wide an arc as possible around the edges of the flock. Renee's anger drained as she watched in fascination how the dog prompted the sheep to their feet and into a rough column. A few times the dog disappeared, only to reappear with two or three sheep moving reluctantly along in front of him. With each passing minute, the man rode farther and farther away and the column of sheep grew longer, until the last one straggled behind the others baaing in protest and running to keep up. The dog trotted up beside the long column, tongue lolling from exertion, though its eyes never strayed from the sheep.

For the first time, Renee realized she had no idea what the man's name was. He looked tough. His movements were easy. She scanned almost straight up the mountainside and then back to the east at the path from which they entered the grassy meadow. With a sinking heart, she realized she had no way of knowing in which direction her home lay.

A rattle in the bushes to her right jerked her attention that direction. Cold fear coursed through her veins and she froze, heart thundering. Snakes would be awake with the warm weather. Or cats. Even bears might be ambling around. Without pausing to think, she dashed off after the band of sheep, running for all she was worth along the edge of the herd, fanning them out off to the side and into the undergrowth. "Help! Please stop."

She sensed whatever lurked behind her moving closer. She imagined that at any moment she'd feel pressure on her back as whatever it was pounced and shoved her to the ground. Her foot caught and she stumbled and cried out.

seven

Tyler heard the cry for help and pulled Sassy around. He scanned the column of sheep and saw where they had plunged off the path and into the rocky ground and dense underbrush. What now? It would take him, Sassy, and Teddy awhile to get the sheep rounded up and back on the trail. With a grunt of displeasure, he backtracked along the column and whistled for Teddy to wait for commands. No use having the dog try to control things until he knew the reason for the girl's distress.

Alert for movement or threat, he frowned when he heard nothing out of the ordinary and saw nothing move. He pulled the Sharps from the scabbard just in case. About two-thirds back along the column of sheep, he spotted the heap on the ground, the elusive hound lying a few feet away, obviously guarding the woman. Apparently the mutt had centered his affections on Renee. His heart rate picked up as he nudged Sassy to a trot, fear rising that Renee had hurt herself. As he drew closer, he heard her sobs. Gut-wrenching cries that scared him with their fierceness. He shot one more distance-eating glance around and slipped the gun into the scabbard. He slid to the ground and knelt beside her, aware that the mutt also chose that moment to disappear into the underbrush. When Tyler touched Renee's shoulder, she didn't move.

"Are you hurt?"

She shook her head, her cries softening.

"Renee?" He wanted to be angry. All he needed now was a hysterical woman to slow down his progress.

"I thought—" He helped her to her feet, and she brushed

at her cheeks. Her knees showed grass stains; her hands were embedded with small gravel. She brushed them together.

"You thought you heard an animal."

She nodded, and the meek vulnerability in her gaze twisted him up inside. He'd seen that look before. That mix of fear and hope. Pleading.

He clicked his tongue and Sassy came up beside them. Without a word, he cupped his hands. Renee needed no further invitation. She settled back as he swung into the saddle. He did his best to shut his mind to her presence, but then his shirt tugged as she grabbed a fistful of the material to hold on to. Tyler swallowed hard and nudged Sassy toward the column of sheep. He whistled and saw Teddy swing into action at the farthest edge of the herd. He shifted Sassy's position to the other side of the herd and began working the sheep forward from the rear of the herd as the dog darted into the underbrush to draw out the sheep Renee's screech and flight had scattered.

Tyler fought hard with every clop of Sassy's hooves to draw his mind back to the sheep and away from the troublesome woman at his back. He scanned for predators and encouraged Teddy to keep the line moving forward. Time passed in a slow wave of receding heat as the sun passed its zenith and began to sink over the tip of the mountain, though he knew daylight would still exist for several hours.

Only when the tightness of his shirt loosened somewhat did he dare hope Renee might be relaxing into the rhythm of Sassy's gait. But, minutes later, the soft, sagging pressure against his back told another story.

He drew rein and shifted in the saddle. "Renee?" Immediately the pressure of her against his shirt released. He couldn't help but smile. "If you fall asleep, you risk falling off."

"I wasn't asleep," she assured, yet the rusty sound of her voice gave her away.

" 'Course not."

"Can I walk?"

Not waiting for an answer, she put her hands on his shoulders and shifted her right leg over. Without a word Tyler turned to brace her and held onto her forearm as she slipped to the ground. "Stay close so you don't spook the sheep again." He watched her begin the trek, taking a place beside Sassy. The nearby sheep shied from her, already having had one experience with her screeches, but he spoke to them, telling them over and over it was okay. Finally, and with no little embarrassment, he used the method that worked best to soothe the animals. The first few notes of song were rough with the nerves he felt singing in front of her. He could feel her eyes on him, but he kept his face forward, leading the herd along like the fabled pied piper.

As the words of the song slipped out, he imagined her exhaustion must match his own. Events of the day spiraled into a tight knot of weariness between his shoulder blades. And still there would be more work to do once they arrived at the new campsite. He finished the song and called out. "We're two miles out."

No answer. He breathed deeply of the cool air and started another song.

Another mile passed before he looked back. Renee still walked, though her stride had diminished to a shuffling stagger toward the back of the long line of sheep. This girl was going to make him crazy. He whistled to Teddy to keep the line going and stopped Sassy to wait for her to catch up. She seemed not to notice his presence and gasped when he planted himself on the ground in front of her.

"You ride," he said, his voice a growl. "I'll walk."

To his surprise she didn't fight him or protest. She leaned heavily on him as he caught her booted foot and raised her up.

"Another mile at most."

Her shallow nod acknowledged his words.

"It won't take me long to set up camp. Then you can sleep."

"Thank you."

At first he thought he'd heard wrong, her voice so low, the words little more than a whisper. "You're welcome, though I'm not sure how thankful you'll be come tomorrow."

If she wondered what he meant, she showed no curiosity. Tyler wondered how long it would take her to come to despise the solitude and crude life of a shepherd. And even as Sassy carried her that last mile to the next camp, he questioned his decision to continue the ride to summer camp with Renee in tow.

eight

Fear tugged Renee toward wakefulness. Thomas's face flared in her mind; then a gunshot rang out and he disappeared. Her breath came hard and fast, her heart beat the thunder of a thousand wild mustangs. She cradled her face and pulled air into her starved lungs. Like someone sawing through ropes with a dull blade, the dream released her one cord at a time. Despite the open sky above her and the light blanket, she expected the face of her captors to appear over her. Taunting. Daring. Thomas, too, his face a mask of pain, accused her.

She became aware, first, of the baaing of sheep. Of the *snap* and *crackle* of a fire. Then of the man who had rescued her.

He sat on the ground two hundred feet in front of her, his back to her. An animal lay in the thick grass beside him. She rubbed at her eyes. His presence cut the last strand of her disorientation. The animal beside him baaed again. She shuffled to her knees, chilled by the sweep of cold against her blanket-warmed skin. He had settled her on the ground and given her a blanket in the early evening of the previous day. She'd slept long and sound, until those last, vivid stabs of memory.

What would she do here? What was there for her? If this man wouldn't take her home, she'd have to find a way to go by herself. But the thoughts filtered away as the sheep's legs stiffened and the animal's neck extended, a powerful *baa* pulsing from its throat. She sat up taller and could see that the man stroked the side of the animal, speaking in low tones, though she could not understand what he said. She watched as he moved, hands gentle on the animal's side.

Mesmerized, she stood to her feet and moved closer. He worked over the animal, sending her a startled glance when he caught sight of her. The animal lay on its side, straining, and Renee realized the sheep was about to give birth. The man motioned her away with a violent slicing of his hand. His dark frown discouraged her even further. She retreated back to the blanket and sat.

He still had his back to her, yet she could see that the birth must be difficult, for the man assisted the animal diligently. The bunching of his shoulders and movement of his head, and above all else, the gentle tone of his voice continued as the long minutes stretched into a ball of tedium. She shifted her position a dozen times, wondering how he could sit so still and be so patient when every nerve in her body pulled taut. Eventually the sheep stretched its neck and pulled almost to a stand. The man sat back on his heels.

When he turned and caught her gaze, he put a finger to his lips. But she glimpsed the burst of a smile as he again faced the new mother and baby. He ran his hand over the newborn animal's face until it wheezed and air filled its lungs. A black lamb. Wet. He lifted it and brought it to the mother, and she began to nuzzle the baby. Renee couldn't take her eyes from the dark form struggling then resigning itself to its mother's nuzzles and licks.

"It's her first lamb." He did not look at her, his eyes on the mother as she cleaned her baby. Something sad slashed across his features. Her heart tugged at the wistfulness in his expression. The sight of mother and child must remind him of family. Way up here, in the mountains, she could see where he would get lonely, perhaps for his own home, wife, and child, for what did she know of him?

"What is your name?"

His eyes flicked over her, euphoria over the lamb's birth morphing into something piercing. "Tyler Sperry."

His gaze held her in its grip until she blinked, confused over the unexpected hostility in the thrust of his jaw and the coldness of his eyes. Before she could respond, or even begin to grasp the reason, he pivoted and waded into the herd. Renee stared after him, feeling more alone than she had in a long time. Weighted by the grief of Thomas's death and her guilt, she curled into a knot by the fire. Hunger bit at the pit of her stomach, but the ache of her loss, of her inability to return home, eclipsed everything else.

Tyler worked among the sheep for hours, checking their feet, patting them as if they were his friends. The sight of him coddling the animals angered her. She needed to go home. How could he worry over such dumb, ugly animals when her need was obviously greater?

The anger burned through her reserve and she burst to her feet, the pinch of placid muscles fueling her anger as she walked about, working the kinks from her back, her gift from sleeping on the hard ground. Her stomach growled, and she railed at Tyler Sperry in her mind for not having at least the sense and hospitality to offer her something.

He continued his work, oblivious to her raging temper and, for the lack of someone on whom to vent her rage, it bled from her in a thin stream that left her exhausted and empty. Not knowing what else to do, Renee plopped down on the ground and hugged her legs to her chest. She buried her head in her arms and must have fallen asleep, for when she lifted her head, she not only felt the heat from a fire but smelled food.

Tyler nudged at something in the skillet then nestled the pan back into the hot coals. He rose to his full height and turned to the crude tent, snatching up a hammer. "Watch the griddle cake while I finish up here. There are a few pieces of salt pork to fry when it's done."

Renee frowned hard. "I'm not a good cook," she bit out. Mama had tried, but nothing Renee put her hand to in the kitchen ever seemed to match what her mother could produce. Or maybe the memories of her mother's cooking were so distorted through years of missing her that she couldn't discern reality from imagination.

"I'm sure you'll do fine."

Heat rose to her cheeks. "Am I to be some sort of slave, then?"

Tyler stood still, his back to her. Her heart slammed hard as she waited for his response. She half expected him to hurl the hammer, but he didn't.

"A little help is always appreciated, Renee."

His soft words flushed her with shame, and her throat ached. "I want to go home."

His head sagged between his shoulders, and she heard his long sigh. "A shepherd doesn't just leave his flock."

She understood. Deep down inside she knew she was being unfair to ask this of him again. "How can I stay here with you? Unchaperoned? It's not. . .right."

"It's not the best situation."

Somehow his concession didn't comfort her. He moved then, toward the tent spread out on the ground and began pounding the stakes. Renee rose to her knees and used a cloth to pull the griddle from the fire. A finger to the top of the griddle cake seemed to indicate it was done. With a fork, she pushed it onto a tin plate. She found the slab of salt pork and sliced some into the griddle, nestling the pan into the hot coals. Settling back on her heels, absorbing the warmth of the fire, she looked up. Tyler's gaze was on her. A small smile curved his lips.

nine

It was the time of day that Tyler usually dreaded, when the loneliness of his occupation ate at him most. Renee's presence seemed odd, yet exciting. What he hadn't realized was that being a sheepherder had chiseled away at his ability to carry a conversation. Or maybe he was just too afraid he'd give himself away. Even mentioning his name had rattled him. He'd feared it would bring instant recognition and fear, something he would expect even if he hated the effect. Regret had become a powerful and very real force in his life.

Tyler stretched out on the ground across from where Renee sat by a pool of water a short distance from the camp. He had debated with himself about interrupting her solitude, but he had questions and she had all the answers.

"Maybe we should talk some more."

He cringed at the way it sounded. Desperate. Awkward. She didn't react, and if his presence irritated her, she didn't show it. Her eyes remained riveted on the smooth surface of the water. Birds flew overhead, chattering and challenging each other. The sheep baaed in the background. Pastoral. Very Psalm 23, Tyler reflected, except for the presence of the woman and the problems it created.

"How did you manage to be taken captive?"

She bowed her head and squeezed her eyes shut.

He regretted the question. Her distress could only mean. . . "Did they hurt you, Renee?"

She sobbed. Once. And then shook her head. "No. Not really. They. . ."

He waited. Knowing something more, darker, must be shadowing her memories.

"It's my fault." Her statement drowned beneath a bank of sobs that shook her shoulders and seemed to rip every bit of strength from her.

He hated the helpless feeling her tears evoked. He glanced at the sheep, incredulous at his earlier vision of pastoral peace. Her tears tinged everything with gray. He was sorry he had rescued her.

No.

That wasn't quite right.

He was sorry he couldn't get her home.

Would they come looking for her? He knew little of the circumstances that placed her with those men. If they were holding her for ransom, they would come after her. If she were a hostage, they might let her go, unless they feared her being able to describe them. In that case they would either run to avoid capture or try to find her trail.

"They shot my brother." Her breaths came hard. He digested the words, fresh anger consuming him. "I wanted him to come with me to find the gang."

"A gang?"

She nodded and brushed her hand across her eyes. "I thought it would be fun. Thomas didn't want to go."

"You thought it would be *fun*?"

"I didn't expect to really find them."

He couldn't believe his ears. This young woman went after a gang because she thought it would be fun? That she'd been foolish to set off after a gang, to even desire such a reckless thing, spotlighted her immaturity. He judged her to be about eighteen. Probably spoiled by parents who demanded nothing of her. If she expected words of consolation, he had none to offer.

"It was a foolish thing you did."

Her eyes flashed to his, angry. "You don't think I know that?"

"Having a person's blood on your hands is a terrible thing."

She swept to her feet, spun, and ran away, scattering the sheep in her path. He let her go. So much for a conversation. But her revelations withered his estimation of her. Still, he'd had his say. He would not coddle whatever insecurity made her go off on such a foolhardy quest and drag her brother along, only to get him killed.

A lamb toddled his way, pausing, its mama close by but its curiosity leading the baby to forget her for a moment. Tyler wondered how many lambs he had rescued in the last three years, their desire to explore their world leading them down a narrow path that separated them and sent their mothers into a frenzy. At least they were innocent of their wrongdoing. Unlike Renee. Unlike himself.

ten

She'd wanted her freedom, curling her lip at the idea of being a wife and mother, of being tied to a ranch and all the hard work when there was a world to see. Places to go and things to do that had nothing to do with horses or saddles, cows or fencing. Thomas would have been alive if not for her. Tyler was right to call her a fool, though it hurt her pride to admit it.

From a safe distance, she watched as he hauled a lamb onto his shoulders and walked it back through the herd to its mother. He knelt by the little one, stroking its head and ears. He went through the flock, touching a random sheep, petting a skittish lamb, or checking the feet of some animal, for what, she didn't know.

He didn't scold them, but his low tones were soothing and gentle even if she couldn't make out his words. He was a strange man. Content to lead a flock of sheep in the middle of nowhere with nothing more than a dog and a tent.

At some point, the wind carried a low humming to her. Tyler was a distant speck, at the lower half of the herd scattered along the meadow. The sheep seemed to enjoy his attention. She tilted her head to catch the source of the humming. A bee? But it was too indistinct beneath the baaing of the sheep and the twitter of birds.

When Tyler had gone through the herd he returned to his spot next to the cook fire and pulled out a small book. Relieved he wouldn't ply her for more answers or want to talk, she studied him from the distance that separated them, realizing she knew nothing of this man who refused to take her back home, or even to a nearby ranch. Instead she was at his mercy. Should she try to leave, she would not get far, not in the rocky terrain, steep slopes, and narrow trails. And the dog, that scarred hound with the tattered ears. . .she shuddered. If Tyler was intent on holding her captive and discovered her missing, he might set the dog on her. She squeezed her head between her hands, desperate with the sudden worry of it all.

"Renee?"

She raised her head, wary. Tyler lifted the little book and gestured to a spot on the ground near him, posing an unspoken question. She shook her head and glanced away, more than content to maintain her distance, even as her hands slid up to rub her arms. The temperature had dropped sharply. The warm fire beckoned her closer.

Her legs were stiff from sitting so long on the large rock. Chilly air bit through her thin blouse, and she ventured a tentative step toward camp. The collie caught her movement and lifted his head. She expected to see his teeth bare, but his intelligent eyes were merely alert, aware for movements out of the ordinary.

Tyler glanced up and motioned her closer again. "You must be cold." With a confidence she didn't feel, she took the next steps.

"It's too cold to wander far from the fire. Tomorrow will be warmer," he said as she drew into the circle of light. He smiled into the sky as if he understood something she didn't. "I can feel it."

"Maybe it's because you're so close to the fire."

Tyler laughed, and the sound reminded her of Thomas. Laughter softened his face and erased the severe expression she'd grown accustomed to seeing. He always seemed so intent on his sheep and his "duty" that her well-being appeared nothing more than a second thought. She winced inwardly.

And why shouldn't it? A sharp wind beat around the hill and pierced through her thin shirt. She shivered.

"No use trying to stay warm out there. Come closer. I'll get a blanket."

She obeyed without protest and angled her body toward the flames. She felt the moment when he lowered the blanket to her shoulders, its weight a welcome shield. In short order he had a pot of something bubbling over the fire. Between the smell wafting from the pot and the warmth, the tightness in her stomach eased. Food sounded good.

A movement to her left caught her eye, and she jumped and turned. Her heart slammed at the shadowy dark figure now crouched next to her before she realized it was Tyler's dog.

"Come here, Teddy," Tyler called. "You know it's supper time, huh?"

Tyler rustled in a sack and threw something. The dog caught whatever it was in his mouth, gave two chomps, and swallowed. She heard Tyler's low chuckle and another piece of food flew through the air.

"Where's the other dog?"

Tyler glanced her way and threw another morsel to Teddy. "You mean the mutt? He kills his own dinner usually. You won't see him much unless there's some trouble he can't handle."

"I saw him on the hill before you got there." She fingered the blanket around her shoulders. "The trail I took down the hillside was the same one he had taken. It was like he was showing me the way."

"He's a good dog. His howls usually mean he's onto a coyote or something, but that day. . ." He shrugged.

"Do you think they'll try to find me?"

Tyler squinted at her, and a hard glint flashed in his eyes. "If they're outlaws."

"I saw the wanted poster on them."

Tyler's nostrils flared. "Outlaws don't like people to interrupt their plans or steal from them, and that's exactly what they would think. But I doubt they'd ever find us. The Big Horns are vast."

Something he had said niggled at her, but she couldn't quite bring it into focus as the fire worked its magic and made her drowsy. She would remember tomorrow.

❧

Tyler didn't sleep well that night, his mind occupied with the dilemma Renee's presence posed and the impact it would have on the safety of the sheep. The woolies seemed more restless than normal, some lying down but most on their feet. One in particular, his boundary walker, found a crevice between two rocks that led to a rough patch with long, dry grass. It took him a while to encourage the ewe back into the pasture. For twenty minutes he worked in the dark to block the crevice by stacking stones.

He meandered back through the herd, noticing that more were on their feet, as if sensing the ewe's escape and fearing they would somehow be in trouble as well. As he strolled in their midst, he hummed, the soft strain of music his gift to them. Tyler stroked the faces of a little lamb and its mother. Their trust in him satisfied on a level he had never experienced.

Not that he'd ever been a man worthy of trust before becoming a sheepherder. What Renee did not know of his past she would be better off not knowing. The girl seemed troubled enough, as well she should be. Still, the death of her brother must weigh heavily on her. He hoped the event would rattle some of her wayward tendencies—setting off after a band of outlaws for fun? He shook his head in the dark, disgusted with her all over again.

As the sky lightened, the sheep began to rise for the morning graze. Teddy went to work at Tyler's command, walking passively along the perimeter of the sheep, ever watchful for those that might stray too far.

Lambs nursed from their mothers as they cropped the lush green grasses of the flat, wide section. His throat grew thick at the idyllic scene, and he wished he could absorb the peace and imprint it on his soul. What he would give to remove the blight his own reckless youth had left. Tyler retreated to the camp and found Renee still asleep. He recognized himself in her. That burning, youthful need for something more. A desire to be different, though unsure of what that difference entailed or what it would cost. Adventure replacing caution and common sense.

He shuffled to the blanket spread on the ground and rolled himself into its warmth. Tyler rummaged in the sack he used as a pillow and pulled out the Bible. He wondered if God could redeem a robbing murderer.

eleven

Renee's eyes snapped open. She became instantly aware of the fire and the man encouraging it to flame higher. The sun was just skimming the horizon, and the sheep baaed as they moved about the grassy area. The picture brought back her mother's stories of serenity and peace. Scriptures she often quoted from the Bible about men in trouble and women who went beyond the edges of what was considered proper. All directed at her. To tame the wild streak that even then her mother had sensed.

She pulled onto an elbow and ran her free hand through the tangles of her hair. She needed to wash it and considered how good it would feel to sink into a tub of hot water.

Tyler poked at something in a pan and put it over the fire. "Got some time before food will be fit for eating."

She nodded and stretched.

"There's a pool of water down a ways if you've a need."

Renee moved in the direction he'd pointed, following the stream as it meandered away from where the sheep grazed. It widened at a point about eight hundred feet away, emptying into a pool deep enough to cover her knees. She gasped at the icy cold clearness and cast an eye back toward camp. She could see the tendrils of smoke rising from the fire but nothing else. If it got hot, the pool would be a refreshing place to bathe and scrub her hair. She raised her hand to scratch at a spot over her ear, chagrined that the idea of washing her hair seemed to make all the itches pop out along her scalp.

With a sigh she lowered herself to the ground, grateful for the material of the trousers covering her knees to protect them from the rough rocks scattered along the shore of the pool. She leaned forward as much as she dared. Her hair swirled in the water but not enough to get wet. With a huff she flipped her hair back and formed a quick twist to secure it with the few hairpins that hadn't slipped out during her captivity and rescue. She would have no choice but to wait until Tyler was out of camp; then she could wade into the pool. Soap, too, would be nice.

When she returned and sat at the fire, Tyler handed a plate over to her. She felt his eyes scan her. "Pool's a good place. Get yourself a cake of soap from my saddlebags. I'll take the sheep down to water after we eat."

She watched as he returned to his spot across from her and sat on his heels, perfectly balancing his weight and the plate of food. He bowed his head for a moment, and she looked down at the food on her own plate wondering what he saw that was so interesting. She scooped up some bacon and chewed, enjoying the rich saltiness of the meat. She'd have to say that the man was a much better cook than she'd ever be. Bacon had been something their cook despaired of having her master.

The thoughts of home, of her father and Thomas, clenched her stomach hard. If Knot Dover didn't love his daughter before he would never love her now that Thomas was dead. She lowered her head, the plate growing blurry as tears collected in her eyes.

She pictured her father's grief-stricken expression, the same one he'd worn since the death of his wife, except this time it would be worn because of Thomas. She wondered if he even missed her. A little voice tried to pry reason into that thought. Her father hadn't always been so remote. She still remembered his tenderness toward her mother. That first time she had caught her father hugging her mother and had laughed out loud at the delight of seeing those two shapes merge to form one big lump. It brought a smile to her lips even as tears squeezed through her eyelids.

Tyler cleared his throat, and she raised her head. He stood a few feet from her, his hands working around the edge of his hat. His downcast eyes showed his awkwardness. "I'll be taking those sheep downstream. Be gone for quite a while." He held out his hand, and a cake of soap sat on his wide palm, a gray-white lump against the roughness of his calloused skin.

She swallowed hard and accepted the gift.

"You can clean up the plates."

She could only nod her head, the urge to protest against the work far away. She didn't know how he cleaned up in a camp, but she'd figure something out.

Tyler said not another word but turned and gathered the reins of his horse, mounting up and whistling for Teddy as he dug his heels into Sassy's sides.

❧

Tyler adjusted his position in the saddle, casting another glance over at the huddled form of Renee Dover. Her rich, thick hair. Her clear skin and smoky eyes. He nudged the horse hard with his spurs. Rich would send a camptender in six more weeks. He would be at summer camp in the mountaintop in two. He'd already given thought to having the man stay with the sheep while he returned Renee home. Six weeks was a long time for the girl to wait. He toyed again with the idea of letting her take Sassy down but knew she would never be able to find the way. He groaned. *Dover, Dover. . .* The name was not familiar, but that didn't mean anything. More people were coming out to the Big Horns every year.

The sheep were lying down. Following a hand signal, Teddy began a slow and wide circle behind the animals. In response to the dog, the sheep rose to their feet and headed off toward the rocky pool a mile downstream. Besides having to bring in

Punky, the wayward ewe who always led a few in rebellion down impossibly narrow paths or out onto ledges, all went smoothly. As the sheep drank of the cool water, lambs, finished with their breakfast milk, began to frolic and play, running and stopping, legs splayed, before they bounced into the air and repeated the actions.

He used the hours with the sheep as a means to give Renee space. As he checked over several of the ever-growing lambs, the sheep spread out more. He rescued a playful lamb that got stuck in brambles. Tyler carried the injured lamb on his shoulders back to the hill that looked out over the stream and sheep. Teddy sniffed at the lamb as Tyler swiped blood from the lamb's cuts and applied a thick salve. When the lamb finally stood on his own legs, the dog nosed the baby and it began bounding around, eventually heading toward a clump of ewes.

Several ewes kicked out at the suckling lamb, refusing to accept its presence as their responsibility. The moment the baby found its mother, the ewe chewed its cud placidly and the baby nursed, little tail flapping in joy. Tyler assessed the two ewes yet to give birth. Most lambs were already thirty days old.

With the herd settled for a while and his long, sleepless night wearing heavily, Tyler stripped off his hat and lay back on the grass, eyes closed against the warm sunshine. His last conscious thought was of glossy dark hair and gray eyes pooling with tears, and of his fingers reaching to wipe those tears from her soft cheek.

twelve

Touching the cool water froze Renee enough to make her scalp prickle. Undeterred, she plunged into the refreshing liquid. The icy cold snapped up her spine. She gasped and splashed, laughing at the spectacle she was making for any animals watching her antics. The water streamed in rivulets down her neck and back and over her shoulders. With brisk strokes she worked the soap over her hair and body, invigorated by the idea of being clean again. Loosening the trail dust with warm bathwater always cheered her back home, though Thomas usually taunted her to "hurry it up" through the curtain that surrounded the wash tub.

The memory of her brother evaporated her joy. She clutched her forearms and pressed her lips together to keep from crying out. *Oh, Thomas.* She dipped her head beneath the water and for a fleeting moment she stayed there, tempted as she'd never been before to inhale and let the water fill her nostrils and lungs. No one would miss her or be disappointed.

A muffled sound caught her attention and brought an immediate picture of a mountain cat to mind. She'd seen only one, and at a distance, but despite the animal's small size, she had also seen the speed with which it moved and the ferocity with which it killed. She jolted upright, squeezing the water from her eyes and pushing her hair back to clear her vision. A bark sounded, and she released a hard sigh. The dog stood in front of her. The mutt with the tattered ears and strange eyes. Pressing a hand over her racing heart, she sank to her knees in the water, too weak to stand.

The dog barked again. Sharp, hard yaps that seemed to send a message she didn't understand.

Her flesh crawled. Had the dog gone mad? His amber eyes appeared sure and steady in their intensity. The dog barked once more. Renee pulled in a steadying breath and swiped the water from her hair then tied it in a loose knot. As she approached the edge of the pool, the dog ran off a few yards, turned around, and sat back down to maintain his watch. But what was he watching for?

She dressed in her still damp clothes, glad she'd washed them first. Chilled to the bone and worried about the dog's strange behavior, she moved. Tyler would know what the dog was trying to communicate, and she suddenly wished she were not alone.

Another bark from the mutt and the animal ran off another few feet, looking over his shoulder as if begging her to follow. "I'm coming, I'm coming."

Her ankle turned on a rock, and she scraped her arm against the surface before she caught herself. As she got to her feet, the dog barked at her again then took off and plunged into the brushy, thorny vegetation.

❧

Tyler awoke with a jolt. The mutt sat down across from him, panting heavily, his yellow eyes alert and staring. Tyler touched his hand to the ground and came to his feet in a smooth motion. He saw that the horse's ears were pricked and she stared hard in the opposite direction.

He yanked the rifle from the scabbard. "Easy, girl." He stroked the horse's neck and mounted, his eyes on the mutt. He gave a sharp, long whistle and Teddy circled off to his left, telegraphing to the sheep that it was time to move. At times like this Tyler wished he had more than one dog to handle the herd, for he knew the mutt's sudden appearance could only mean the sheep were in danger.

The tatter-eared dog leaped through the air at a run, diving into the underbrush. Tyler could trace his path by the occasional fluttering of the underbrush.

And that's when he heard it. The scream. Tyler gripped the rifle as his eyes roved the rocky outcroppings to his right, the direction in which Sassy was looking. The mountain rose almost perpendicular, a climb he knew he would have to make over the next couple of days. The mountain lion would be up there, more than likely, eyeing the sheep and sizing up the kill. Sassy's ears swiveled back and forth. Steady as the horse was in a crisis situation, the one thing Sassy had no fondness for was mountain cats. He tightened his hold on the reins and patted the horse's neck.

He glanced at the sheep. Teddy knew his stuff and worked the sheep with a calm confidence that reassured rather than frightened. Those ewes that had wandered away from the main body of the flock were loping out of the woods and over toward the majority.

Tyler noted two things—the oddity of a cat prowling at this time of day and the desperation that must be driving it to do so. Neither bode well for the flock. The mutt would instinctively go after the cat—had, in fact, probably sensed it long ago. Tyler made his decision and raised his head to release a warbling whistle directing Teddy to move the sheep forward. Then he nudged Sassy forward. They skimmed the far edge of the flock at a fast walk as Teddy began pushing the sheep away from the water back to the bedding ground of the previous night. A mile away. But they could spread out there, and there was a rise where he could see for miles in every direction.

Renee!

Her name struck fear. There would be no way to alert her. Nothing he could do but hope she at least knew the danger when she heard the cat's distinctive scream. If she stayed near the fire she would be fine. He spurred Sassy into a canter.

Punky tried to push away with about ten other sheep, but Tyler cut them off and got them turned while Teddy worked to keep the other side of the column in line. Tyler kept a sharp eye on the rocky ledge overhead as the sheep moved, expecting at any moment to see a cat leap down onto the helpless back of some woolie.

Short, sharp barks rang out, followed by another low scream from the cat. Tyler brought his rifle up and sighted down the barrel. Nothing moved on the ledge. He heard the mutt growl low in his throat. Tyler's heartbeat skittered upward. Every muscle in his body tightened, and he longed for the sight of the cat, knowing how vulnerable his herd would become should the mutt get killed. He'd lasted through some tough battles with rattlers and coyotes, but a cat. . .

A sickening mewling, gravelly with menace, rose and fell as the two animals squared off. The dog's barks, consistent and fierce, were sharp and harsh, not as high pitched as usual.

Tyler measured his options. The mountain lion would do its best to scare off his unexpected opponent with a series of snarls. The mutt, though, would be no match for a cat. Tyler had but minutes to make his move.

He traced the path up to the ledge with his eyes. Scaling it would take too long. He lowered the rifle and stabbed glances at the rocks surrounding him. Boulders lay along the path of the stream. With a modicum of strides he pushed Sassy toward the farthest boulder, dismounted, and skipped to the lowest of a trio of boulders. Using them as stepping-stones, he clawed and pulled until he stood on the biggest. He raised his gaze as he settled the rifle, gratified to have a clear view of the ongoing battle. But his new dilemma slammed into his gut as he viewed the scene. The cat had the higher elevation to his advantage, with the dog holding lower ground, legs braced wide, showing his teeth, eyes locked with those of the cat's.

Tyler raised the gun to his shoulder and took careful aim. To miss would mean pandemonium. His finger tensed on the trigger just as the cat sprung toward the dog. Tyler lowered the gun to gauge the fight and the dog's chances, helpless to do anything now that the two animals were engaged. He swallowed hard against the burn in his throat.

He had always known the mutt to be a sweet animal, though he'd seen it fight, coming alive with the rage and instincts to kill of his ancestors. The mutt enjoyed his job as guardian of the herd. Rich Morgan had trained the animal well.

The cat rolled the dog to its back and took a swipe at its neck only to roar with anger and draw back when the dog kicked out with its hind feet and lowered its jaws on the cat's nose. Back and forth the battle went. Blood ran from a deep gash in the dog's shoulder. Tyler raised the rifle to his shoulder again, steeling the trembling in his hands to make his aim more sure. The animals would tire of the fight and break apart. He had to be ready for that moment.

The hound rolled the cat down a rocky incline and the animals both scrambled for their footing, placing them a few feet apart. Tense with the opportunity, Tyler tightened his finger on the trigger and the gun fired. A howl rent the air. For a minute the air was heavy with silence. Tyler sucked air into his lungs and took aim again at the cat. The shot found its mark. Writhing and twisting, the animal fought the new, invisible enemy for seconds before pushing to its feet, only to fall to the ground again and lie still.

Hands shaking, Tyler felt the coldness of shock begin to take hold of his body. He fought it and pushed to his feet, moving while the opportunity allowed and before he could think about what he'd just done. He had eradicated the enemy. But there was no sign of the dog, and his mind painted the picture of what the howl after his first shot meant.

thirteen

Renee saw the column of sheep, their bleats filling the air as they made their way in her direction. They fanned out as the narrow trail broadened, but the momentum of the sheep behind them pushed those in front. Minutes passed as the sheep galloped onto the ground just outside the campsite. The rear of the column came into view, with Teddy weaving back and forth behind the herd, keeping them moving. She expected to see Tyler, but he was nowhere.

A terrible, scratchy scream shattered the clamor of the sheep's hooves against the trail and dulled the baaing of the animals. She knew that sound for what it was. She wondered if the tatter-eared dog had sensed the animal's presence and come to her at the pool as a means of warning her.

She stood frozen, eyes scanning, not daring to leave the sputtering fire even for a minute. Above the din created by the milling sheep, she thought she caught the sound of snarling. A shot rang out, and she tensed and clasped her hands around her knees, curling tighter into a knot, unsure what to do. Never again would she allow the man to leave her without at least the protection of a gun. She hated the fact that she didn't know where Tyler was or the reason he discharged his rifle.

In tense silence she waited for the inevitable return of Tyler, or the mutt. Teddy trotted to camp and sank to the ground, tongue lolling with the effort of his herding. She stooped to scratch the dog's head.

"What's going on out there, Teddy?"

The dog stared at her, ears pricked.

Her throat knotted with fear. If anything happened to Tyler she wouldn't even know how to survive or where to go. Her sole hope would be the arrival of the man Tyler had called the camptender.

She squeezed her eyes shut and rested her forehead on her folded arms. Her mind churned with the possibility of being attacked by a bear. She would have to gather wood to keep a fire going to fend off wild animals. The sheep, though. . . She didn't know what they needed or what to do for them. She'd heard Tyler whistle to the dog on several occasions, each whistle apparently meaning something different to the animal.

Her head began to pound, and she pushed against the tears that burned for release. Another thought taunted. What if Tyler had been hurt and couldn't move? She lifted her head, the idea sending waves of panic coursing through her body. She swept to her feet and knelt by the saddlebags and the pack that seemed to hold so many of the necessary staples. Surely the man carried something for wounds.

Renee pulled items out one by one. A bag of beans. Flour. Sugar. Coffee. She dug deeper and discovered a salted ham. The other bag held personal items. Books. The Bible she'd seen him read on the previous day. A clean shirt and trousers. Strips of leather and clean patches of cotton material. A tin of a thick cream that she raised to her nose. Some type of salve, she hoped.

She took the cotton material and began ripping it into strips, rolling them as fast as her stumbling fingers could manage. She tied the leather around the rolls of cotton and jammed the salve into the middle of the last cotton strip before she rolled that, too, into a tight wad.

She would need water, but she gave up the idea of hauling the heavy pail. She would have to move him to water. But if his injuries prevented him. . .

Renee shook her head, gathered her treasures into her arms, and turned. If she didn't add more wood to the fire it would burn out and leave her without a place to retreat for safety.

She dropped her cache of bandages onto a grassy patch, her gaze shifting over the wide space in front of her. A small grove of trees offered some possibilities. She glanced around for the small hand ax she'd seen Tyler use on many occasions but couldn't find it. She used a long wooden stick to poke at the fire and threw on another log. The last one. She could only hope that the flame wouldn't consume the dry wood before she could get Tyler back to the campsite. If she could get him back.

She turned at the dull vibration of the earth. Squinting in the direction from which the sheep had come, she saw a small dot of movement. Relief rolled over her when she recognized Sassy, with Tyler sitting upright on the horse. She strained to make out his features, afraid to see them pinched with the pain of a wound. She ran out as Sassy came closer, slowed to a trot now by Tyler's guiding hand. He raised his hand to her. Anxiety peeled away.

"I was afraid you were injured."

Tyler stopped the horse, his brow pinched with something she could not define. "Guess you heard the cat."

"I heard the shots," she admitted, her body quivering with relief so powerful she feared she might fall in a heap.

He said nothing as he dismounted, pulling the reins over Sassy's head and leading her through the sheep to a boulder where he picketed the horse and removed the saddle and blanket. He gave the horse a pat on the neck.

His silence stoked her temper to a white-hot flame. How dare he ignore her. She retreated to the fire, miserable that she'd burned so much energy worrying over a man not the least bit troubled by all the turmoil he'd caused her. She glared at him as he moved among the sheep, oblivious to her.

She poked at the fire; the flames caught at the old wood and leaped up a few inches. He cared more for the sheep than he did for humans. It was absurd. How could she be expected to stay in this camp for who knew how long with a man who couldn't see beyond the end of his own nose?

She flopped onto the ground and drew her legs up to her chest. As the flames grew in height, she refused to move back. She was hungry, too. She stabbed another glare at Tyler's back as he ran his hands over some of the sheep searching for what, she didn't know.

He worked over the sheep for what seemed an eternity. Lulled by the heat, Renee never noticed when he returned, awakened by the sound of grease in a pan and the smell of something delicious.

When she blinked her eyes open, it was dark, and Tyler sat across the fire from her, his Bible spread on his lap, his expression far away. Without moving she studied his face, noting the crease on his forehead that showed tan beneath it and paler skin above, a product of Tyler's preference to wear a hat as he worked. For the first time she realized his face was not that of an old man. Her best guess put him in his late twenties. Creases at the corners of his eyes spoke of a man who squinted or laughed often, though she suspected the former as he'd only once cracked a smile since her arrival.

And again she had to ask herself the question. What kind of man secluded himself away in the mountains of Wyoming for months on end with nothing but sheep, a horse, and two dogs for company?

❧

Tyler felt her eyes on him. She'd awakened at some point between the memory of his wasted youth and his moment of redemption. If, indeed, that moment had come at all. Maybe it never would. The Bible in his lap nudged him to cling to the hope of a better day. A new day. And it reminded him of the sheep.

He rubbed his hands together, distributing the oil on them from the new growth of the sheep's wool, which was still short since they'd just been clipped. If he'd known at the age of seventeen what he would be doing at twenty-six, he would have laughed. Much as he suspected Renee laughed at the idea of being in the mountains, alone with a herd of sheep and a hard-edged, silent man. His silence upon his return had irritated her, he was sure, but he'd needed time.

Sheepherding had been a way for him to cut himself off from all the painful things he'd done—to himself and to others. He'd welcomed the retreat into the mountains offered to him by Rich Morgan, a rancher who'd taken a chance on a broken-spirited man with no heart for living another day.

Rich had told him his wound wouldn't kill him, but his broken spirit would grind him to dust if he let it. Despite Tyler's desire for death, Rich had helped Tyler's body along the path of healing. And then Rich had offered him a stake in a herd of sheep and sent him up into the mountains. Tyler had spent the first month of that first trip surrounded by more silence than he could take, thinking he would go crazy with nothing but the sheep and the sheepdog for company. He'd been forced to leave Sassy at the ranch to heal.

"She'll be needing some extra care," had been Rich's argument. "That shoulder wound is pretty deep. She's too good a piece of horseflesh to let her go lame."

Tyler had set out on the trail up the mountain with no illusions about the job, having heard too many stories from the other herder Rich employed. Rich had turned up at the end of that month, checking on the herd, he'd said, but Tyler suspected the man was checking up on him as well as the herd.

It had been on the tip of his tongue many times to bark his complaints, but Rich's kindness to him, and his compassion and willingness to help a stranger at a time when Tyler had felt himself beyond help or hope, meant he could not let his friend down. Plus the herd was his investment. All the money he had was wrapped up in the timid little animals.

Tyler pulled himself from the wrappings of memory and set the Bible aside. Renee watched him in silence, though he couldn't be sure that she wasn't watching the flames. He got to his feet and stuck the fork into the chunk of meat in the pan. The water was simmering it slowly, making a nice broth in which to boil the beans that he'd left soaking that morning.

"I'm hungry," were her first words.

He nodded. "It'll be awhile. Take some coffee."

He filled a tin mug for her.

"Sugar?"

A precious staple, sugar. He preferred to drink his black, but if sugar soothed the lady. . . He spilled some from the large sack into another tin mug and took it back to her. She dumped most of it into the coffee and swirled it around.

At least sipping the brew would keep her occupied until supper. Good thing since he had more work to do.

"That dog barked at me."

Tyler lifted his gaze to hers then glanced over at Teddy, who lounged at the edge of the herd.

"Not that one. The one with the fringed ears."

He frowned, unsure of the direction of the conversation. Could it be that she resented the dog barking at her, perhaps scaring her? "He does that to get your attention."

"I heard the cat later on." She sipped at the coffee, made a face, and dumped in the last of the sugar. "Was he warning me, do you think?"

The mutt had a sixth sense about danger. There had been so

many times when Tyler hadn't heard or sensed anything amiss with the herd but the mutt had. He'd often taken off under cover of dense shrubs, guarding the sheep as if they were his own pups. "Probably."

"You don't talk much, do you?"

He nodded her way. "Don't mean to be rude. Guess I'm not used to having company."

"You shot the cat?"

"In the neck or head."

"Did the dog find him?"

"Found him and picked a fight. It was a young cat but it outweighed the hound." He squinted out toward the sheep. He would need to set some fires around the perimeter of the herd to help keep predators at bay. He'd shoot a rabbit for Teddy while he was out. "Keep an eye on the meat. Beans are soaking over in that pan. Add them and put a lid on it. Should be back by the time they're done cooking."

fourteen

The sheep seemed calm despite the extra movement brought about by the presence of the cat. Tyler winced at the memory. How could he have missed the cat that first time? His hands must have been trembling more than he realized. He'd nailed it with the next shot, though, even as the reality of what his first shot had cost him sunk deep into his mind.

It had taken him awhile to climb the incline where the mountain lion lay dead within a few feet of the mutt. Mercifully he'd shot the dog in the chest, its howl probably the last sound its starved lungs could gasp. He'd dug a shallow hole with a sharp-edged rock and buried the animal, agonizing over the loss. Rich Morgan wouldn't be too happy with him, but the man would read the situation for what it was and hold no blame.

At least the mutt had sired a litter of pups the past winter. They'd be old enough to train by summertime. The loss of the dog cut deep for numerous reasons. Tyler put complete trust in the animal's instincts to track and keep predators away from the herd. It meant he would have to be more on guard. Ever watchful in his hearing as well as his vision, and even then his instincts would never be as refined as the hound's.

He scrambled together some twigs and leaves and used them as kindling for the small fires. He crossed between the four that he set, working them until they were hot enough for the greener wood that would produce smoke.

When he returned to the camp, he gave the rabbit to Teddy. Renee sat cross-legged, peeling the bark off a twig one strip at a time. He passed her without comment, understanding all too well the boredom she must be feeling. Getting involved working the sheep would be good for her. Time would fly faster if she had chores and responsibilities.

He bent over the pot, satisfied to see the beans had been placed inside as he had requested.

"Were you afraid I would forget?"

Her voice held an edge. He ignored the question. "I'll get the plates." When he handed her a plate, she took it, her eyes searching his. He met her gaze head on, unwilling to let whatever attitude that brewed go unchecked. "Work will be good for you, you know. It will pass the time, and with the loss of the dog. . ."

❧

Renee lifted her eyes from the plate of beans and the strip of meat. Tyler's words sank in slowly, and there was no missing the catch in his voice. "The dog? You mean the mangy one?"

Tyler ran a hand over his mouth, the material of his sleeve catching on the coarseness of his stubbled chin. "Shot him by mistake."

As far as she could see, the loss of the dog wasn't anything that terrible.

"He was a fine animal. Brave. Smart. Could track a coyote and kill a rattler in an instant. And his loss means more work. I don't have him to drive away predators, which leaves the sheep more vulnerable."

It was the longest stream of words she'd heard from him. "Why do you do this? Get stuck out here? For them? Doesn't it make you crazy?"

Tyler's eyes glittered in the firelight, and she thought she saw a slight smile curve his lips. "I felt the same way the first month. Rich kept telling me to pay attention to nature and I wouldn't be bored. Then he gave me a Bible."

Renee's laugh was harsh. "Did you get religion or something?"

He seemed to mull her question, taking a bite of beans. "I don't know what happened. Things change so much. The sky, for example—have you ever paid attention to it? The colors?"

A laugh rose in her throat, but the sincerity with which he spoke made mirth seem folly. He was serious.

"The sheep are gentle creatures. I hated them at first. Thought they were dumb animals." He paused and stared out at the flock.

"What changed your mind?"

"It was all about me. I hated being up here. I hated being alone. I hated them because they were the reason for my isolation."

Renee let his words sink in, unsure what it all meant. "Then why come at all?"

"Because I had no choice."

fifteen

At first, she couldn't think of anything to say. Ideas that explained his reason for becoming a sheepherder rolled around in her mind. Maybe he'd been jilted by a girl. He'd said he blamed the sheep for his isolation, but how could that be?

He shifted his weight, and the flames of the fire caught the strong cut of his jaw. His eyes seemed paler in the brightness. His expression always appeared on the brink of becoming surly and hard. She shivered at the idea of feeling the heat of his anger. She set aside her plate, hunger dulled by the hardness of the beans. She would have to add them sooner next time.

Tyler had never been anything but a gentleman. Terse, perhaps, but what man wasn't when working hard at a job? Her pa never had much to say when there was work to be done, which was why the evenings seemed such a special time for her as a child. At least, before her mother had died.

When he spooned the last of the beans into his mouth, he pushed to his feet. "If you'll wash the plates, I'll check the herd one more time."

"What do you mean that you had no choice?" She blurted out the words, curiosity overwhelming her. She'd had a choice to drag Thomas into her little schemes, never considering the consequences of those actions. Surely Tyler had more options open to him than being a shepherd.

He stopped in his tracks and turned. His hand scratched along his jaw then fell to his side. "Some make bad choices. Others make good. It's all about what we learn from our experience. You're not the only one to make a bad choice,

Renee. And if that group that caught you does find us, we'll have to make some more choices. Real fast."

Tyler turned and walked off. She bit her lip and picked up the dirty plates, never having considered the danger she put him in if the Loust Gang found them. Kneeling by the bucket of water, she used an old rag to rinse the plates, eyes lifting along the herd of sheep, content and peaceful.

❧

Renee Dover was a troubled girl. The desire to draw her out both surprised and annoyed him. Getting involved in the girl's problems wasn't his business. Teddy waded with him into the midst of the sheep. Tyler stilled and listened hard for sounds of predators. As if in answer to his unspoken question, a coyote howled, and a series of yips answered. Tyler gave a grim smile. Most of the sheepherders in the region would have taken note of those sounds. These were far off. About a mile by his guess. It was the silent stalkers, bears and cats, that raised the hair on the back of his neck.

He checked his smoke screens and relit one that had gone out. The smoke was feeble at best, but it was all he could do tonight. Weary from the day, Tyler left Teddy at the edge of the pool and stripped down. The cold water shattered his weariness and sharpened his mind. He worked the soap over his back and down his arms. He scrubbed the bar over his head and down his face. If he'd given it more thought he would have brought his razor and shaved off the scrubby bush. He'd do it in the morning. Lingering in the pool of water in the dark was risky with it being a perfect watering hole for the very predators he hoped to avoid. Tyler left the cold water reluctantly, invigorated, but anxious to get back to the warmth of the fire.

Teddy growled low in his throat, and Tyler hurried into his trousers and poked at the sleeves of his shirt. He knew better than to leave camp without his rifle, and his detour to bathe was more than foolhardy when unarmed.

Whatever had alerted Teddy moments ago didn't seem to bother him now. Tension ebbed from Tyler's shoulders and he hastened back to camp, not bothering to tuck his shirt.

The sheep were quiet, and Teddy curled up in his spot overlooking the herd, ready in an instant to splash into the midst and get them moving.

"Good boy, Teddy."

He patted the dog and scrubbed his fingers down through the thick fur to scratch at his rump, an attention Teddy particularly loved. From his vantage point beside the dog, he looked into camp, expecting to see Renee. When he couldn't make out her form anywhere within the ring of light, his breath caught.

"Renee?" he whispered.

He stalked the perimeter of the fire, keeping his face away from the bright light lest he ruin his night vision. Her bedroll lay on the ground where she'd left it that morning. The plates were gone, the skillet beside the fire where he'd left it. He told himself not to panic. He would embarrass her and himself if he traipsed after her only to discover she'd left to take care of personal needs.

He squatted beside the fire and held out his cold-stiffened fingers. Time weighed heavy on his mind. He kept expecting her to step into the camp, plates in hand. Duty done. He stood, buttoned his shirt, and stuffed it into his pants. He would not wait another minute. He grabbed his rifle and marched to the perimeter of the camp, not quite willing to leave just yet. Renee obviously needed schooling in camp life. She should never leave camp at night unless she took the rifle or Teddy. The irony that he'd violated his own rule made him clench his teeth hard. He moved into the stretching shadows. Something skittered out from beneath a shrubby patch to his right. Tyler tensed, but the small animal scurried away.

He gave a low, quiet whistle, and Teddy loped to his side. The collie was not a guard dog, but the sensitivity of his eyes and ears could mean the difference between life and death.

Night sounds seemed loud now, taunting him with his inability to find the girl. He'd never been fond of wandering the mountains at night. Too many risks. He tightened his hold on the rifle. He didn't do vulnerable.

Teddy went still, his head cocked, ears pricked. Seconds passed. Tyler wished the moon would show its face, but the thick clouds seemed slow to scoot. He heard a new sound. Slow. A creeping *whoosh* that exploded his chest. The sheep were moving, panicked by an enemy. A scream rent the air.

Sweat broke out on Tyler's forehead as he tried to remain steady and grip the direction of the sound, sure this time the sound was not the ladylike scream of a mountain cat, but Renee.

"Renee!"

Teddy lunged forward, a blur of white moving along the edge of the herd. The sheep were bunching away from the threat. Tyler raised the rifle to his shoulder as a panicked whimper rent the air.

"Renee!"

He could make out her outline now. Another dark blur moved behind her. Loping along. The sheep broke into a run. Tyler aimed the gun at the blur behind Renee, sucked air into his lungs, and then pulled the trigger. The animal growled and kept moving. He shot again, and then again. Rage-filled roars filled the air, and the dark mass fell and remained still.

Tyler stabbed through the dark to find Renee's figure. He saw nothing. "Renee?"

"Here." Her voice trembled. "I'm here."

Teddy bounded out of the darkness. Tyler whistled and the dog took off. Tyler's limbs shook with the shock of the ordeal. He found Renee on the ground, head in her hands. He heard the deep sobs that wrenched through her and knelt beside her. "Hey." She shuddered a breath. "I forgot to tell you to take the rifle when you leave camp. Or Teddy."

She didn't answer, the sobs clawing out of her. He touched her shoulder, and she raised her head. He wasn't sure who moved first, but she was in his arms then, her back shuddering beneath his hand.

As they sat there the sheep returned. Slow, spooked, more bunched than normal. But his presence seemed to soothe them and they began to spread out again. And still he held the fragile form in his arms, unable to let go though her tears were spent, her terror diminished.

sixteen

Renee clung to him. His presence something secure and stable. His solid strength pushed her fears back to manageable proportions, and still she couldn't make herself let go. Didn't want to move away from the safety of his arms or the beating of his heart that soothed with evidence she was not alone.

If it hadn't been for him, the bear would have killed her. She'd wanted to die earlier, at the pond, even welcomed it, but instincts for survival had made her run from the bear. If she hadn't looked up and seen it lumbering down off an outcropping, probably coming for water but having its eye on the sheep, she would never have made it. And if Tyler hadn't been there with the rifle. . .

She shuddered and his arms tightened around her.

"Let's get you closer to the fire," he whispered into her ear.

She nodded against his shoulder and pulled from his embrace. As he helped her to her feet, she felt the muscles in her ankle protest.

"Lean on me if you need to."

Renee shook her head. "I've been enough trouble already. I can walk."

He didn't argue but neither did he let go as he led the way back to camp, Teddy joining them at some point. He patted the dog's head and scratched its rump. The campfire burned low for lack of fresh fuel. Renee lifted a log as big around as her leg and lugged it toward the fire. Sparks shot up into the air when she dropped it, and Tyler laughed.

Turning to him, she pressed her hands to her hips. "What?"

"You'll have to get something a little smaller to build the fire up first." With that he grabbed a few slender branches and broke them with his hands into short lengths. He used the long stick to roll the heavy log off the fire and placed the smaller branches on top. The flame caught the dry sticks immediately.

"I have a lot to learn."

Tyler nodded. "We all do."

"I guess my first lesson is not to wander at night."

He shrugged, and a slight smile seemed to play at the corners of his mouth. "Wandering at night is sometimes necessary. The lesson is not to do it without a gun or dog."

She stared down at her fingers, cramped from the cold, her palms bloody from her fall, and she realized when Tyler turned away that his shirt showed stains from her hands. She shuddered. Terror tightened her throat. The bear had moved more swiftly than she had anticipated.

"Lesson two."

Tyler's soft voice brought her attention back to him.

"Don't run from a bear. Your best bet is to scream and flail your arms until the bear backs off. If that doesn't work, drop down and pull yourself into a knot."

"And wait to be eaten."

This tugged a smile from him. It transformed his face and lit his eyes.

"You should smile more often."

His smile wilted, and she wished she could take the words back.

He glanced away. "We need to be getting some sleep. I was going to shift the animals off, but the grass is holding so we'll stay put tomorrow."

She had no idea what all that meant, but he didn't explain further and she didn't want to ask more questions. Her body seemed to deflate all at once and it was all she could do to roll out the blankets and crawl into their warmth before drifting away into velvet slumber.

❧

Tyler lay awake long after she slept, troubled by his reaction to the woman. She tugged at emotions he hadn't felt for a long time. Hadn't wanted to feel. Renee wasn't his type. Their embrace had been nothing more than a means to soothe her overwrought nerves. But her observation about his smile was different. It both pleased and embarrassed him. He'd not thought of himself as attractive since Anna.

He rolled away from the fire and onto his back. Anna had just begun to love him. The few times they'd been together had been magic. She would have been everything his mother would have loved in a daughter-in-law. For Anna he would have given up the wayward life and become someone she could respect. He had been ready to do just that, too.

Renee was none of the things Anna was. She was younger, for one thing, more. . . What? Selfish? Who was he to judge? But she'd suffered. Something haunted the girl, and he wanted to drag it from her. Talking about the deep down things had helped him. Rich Morgan had been a patient friend. He could do the same for Renee, but he had no inkling of how to do that. He was no healer, and his best attempts with talking to people proved clumsy.

It would be so easy to ignore her. He could use her help in camp. It would be good for her to be busy, just as he'd suggested to her, but he wouldn't get involved.

He closed his eyes, settled on the matter, but sleep wouldn't come. The feel of her in his arms. The frailty of her frame beneath his hand. The harshness of her sobbing gasps. A longing for a closeness he'd denied himself came alive despite his efforts to the contrary.

seventeen

Renee woke up shivering. The crackle of fresh wood on the fire beckoned her closer. She climbed out, gasped at the chill air, scooted her blankets closer to the heat, and dove back inside.

Rich, male laughter made her squeeze her eyes harder.

"Playing possum won't work. Breakfast is almost ready anyway."

She wiggled her toes and debated abandoning her blankets to help with breakfast.

"I could leave it for the bears."

Renee lifted the covers over her head.

"I'm sure they'll come running when they see you, their old friend."

He wasn't going to leave her alone, but she had to admit that the sparkle of humor in his words delighted her. Even his rare burst of laughter seemed a gift. She swept the covers back in a pretend huff, immediately wishing she hadn't been so hasty when the cold air slammed against her.

"Do you have those plates?"

"I'll get them." She stretched her body upward and tried to tame her hair. Tyler stood, drawing her attention and making her gasp. It was Tyler, but it wasn't Tyler. He caught her stare and ran a hand over his jaw.

"Tired of looking scruffy. Meant to do it last night."

The line of tan skin beneath where his hat rested on his head grew pale again along the newly shaven jaw and chin. But the clean-shaven face peeled years away. Despite the strange coloring of his skin, Tyler was a handsome man. His lips full.

A cleft in his chin. Square jaw. She gasped air, not realizing she'd been holding it as she perused his new look. "You—you look. . ." *Handsome* was the word she almost spit out, but she clamped down and finished with an awkward, "younger."

"How old did you think I was?"

Renee glanced away, heat creeping into her cheeks. "Late twenties. Early thirties." She hugged herself, remembering, against her will, how he had held her in his arms and what protection and comfort truly felt like. She'd had too few of the latter in her life, and a gun was generally her protection. "Let me go get those plates."

His chuckle caught her attention. "I'll get them while you finish waking up."

She watched him lift down the plates then turn, catching her eye, his expression serious. Sober. She didn't know what to think about him or about the feelings he stirred. Was it wrong for her to enjoy the comfort he so freely had given during a moment of crisis? She didn't think so. He had saved her life.

His eyes slid away from her gaze, and he picked up a paper-wrapped piece of meat. "The bear left us with a few good things."

This surprised her. "How long have you been up?"

His grin went huge. "Longer than you."

"If you'll show me how, I'll try and do the cooking."

"Your mama never taught you?"

His casual assumption rattled something deep down. "She died when I was eight."

"I'm sorry."

There it was. Simple comfort. His tone conveyed a deep empathy. She stared out at the herd, moving now in the cold gray of morning light. Peaceful. Quiet.

" 'The Lord is my Shepherd.' " Her heart raced at the voice, and she thought for a moment that God Himself was speaking to her. Tyler, his face turned toward the grazing sheep, too, continued, as if reading her thoughts. But she recognized the words of someone else entirely. "'I shall not want.'"

He didn't continue, and in the stillness Renee heard her mother's voice; she'd often quoted that psalm late in the evening. Her father had been there, too, listening as she read, a tender smile lighting his eyes as he would pull her closer to him. Renee hadn't recalled those nighttime Bible readings in years.

As a child she had accepted the words because they were read by the mother she loved so much. When had she begun to doubt? She knew the answer. Her mother's death. The change in her father had been jarring. He began to shuffle her and Thomas off to neighbors when he had a cattle drive. She hated every minute of being away from him, plied from his side for reasons she didn't understand and had stopped trying to figure out long ago. How she wished for someone to take care of her with the same tenderness with which Tyler cared for his sheep.

"You're their shepherd."

He rubbed his jaw, as if he couldn't quite get enough of the smooth feel of his skin. "I suppose I am."

She made a face. "You didn't know?"

"I don't think about it much. I do what needs to be done to keep them content."

"You *are* a religious man, then?"

❧

The way Renee said it gave him pause. Did he read the Bible? Yes, but he read other books, too. Did that make him religious? Caring for the sheep had begun as a job. He realized now that it was a calling, one he'd been ill equipped to take on at first, but something he had grown into. That first month he'd resented the position, resigned to being alone because it was his safeguard against those who would seek him out.

"I began to see the sheep for what they were. Helpless, dependent animals who needed care and attention." His throat closed over the words, and he dipped his head beneath Renee's gaze. Waxing poetic about sheep seemed silly.

"You mean you enjoyed bossing them."

He wanted to laugh, but she hit too close to the truth. Though bossing wouldn't have been the word he would have used, it would have appeared that way to anyone watching him at the beginning of his training. "Bossing doesn't have anything to do with it. You lead sheep, you don't beat them. I found it was less about me and my needs and more about responsibility than anything else. Like I said, you just do what needs done because it needs doing." He paused to gather his thoughts. "Some sheep aren't easily led. They get it in their head to bolt off every chance."

Renee moved beside him back to the camp, her silence weighing on him, until, finally: "I guess there are a lot of us like that."

He didn't respond. He understood the deeper meaning of her words all too well. For a second, he considered sharing his story. It would prove to her how far he'd come, or at least, how far he felt like he'd come since his wild youth.

In camp, Renee picked up the heavy iron skillet and sliced some of the meat into the pan. Her hands worked in jerky motions. To his eye she seemed upset, but he refused to pry. Could be she was thinking of her brother or missing her folks. Lord knew even though he was a grown man, he still missed his ma and pa.

"What now?"

Her question startled him, and when he met her gaze, her expression seemed more relaxed. He nodded toward a small sack. "Flapjacks. I'll show you how."

Days settled into a familiar rhythm. Renee's cooking did nothing to aid his digestion, but she was learning and he refused to criticize. Besides, he'd eaten worse many times. The task of herding the sheep up the mountain to summer camp became easier now that he had help, and he enjoyed showing Renee the right way to work with sheep; all the lessons he had learned along the way. At least most of them. At night he would set the small fires and return to camp to whatever Renee had cooked up. She hadn't said much over the last few days, and he hadn't prodded. With days beginning at three in the morning, conversation became a luxury neither indulged in, too tired at night to find words.

But he enjoyed watching her work, and the gentle hand she had with the sheep was rewarded by their trust in her. Where once they had run when they saw her coming, now they calmed and skirted around her, vying for attention.

The last leg of the journey led through patches of dense sagebrush on a narrow ledge. Getting the sheep through would be the challenge it was every year. That night he made a point of opening a conversation, lonely with the silence between them and needing to outline his plan for the next day.

"You've been quiet."

Renee's spoonful of stew didn't make it to her mouth. She set the spoon down. "I didn't think you were much for talking."

He shrugged. "Guess silence has become second nature to me."

"Is the camptender going to arrive soon?"

The question pierced him. So she was only biding her time. He'd thought she might be coming to enjoy tending the sheep, maybe even enjoying. . . What? A silent man incapable of reading a woman's heart and mind? Irritated, he snapped, "He'll get here!"

Renee's eyes flashed. She bit her lip and looked away. "My father. . ."

Whatever she'd been about to say was lost. The strength of her emotion was evident in the way her jaw worked and her lips tightened. She angled her face away from him, toward the night sky. The campfire danced along her cheek and neck but left her eyes in shadow.

"He'll be looking for you."

"No." Her shoulders sagged and she pulled her knees to her chest and rocked. "He probably hates me."

To his ears the words were raw with emotion. "Not as much as you hate yourself."

She was shaking her head, and he heard the tears in her voice. "With Thomas gone he'd have no one. . . ." She shrugged. "It was to be an adventure. I'd gone to town and seen the poster and thought it would be fun to search for the outlaws. Thomas didn't want to go."

It was the perfect time to ask, yet Tyler didn't know if he was ready for the answer. Still, there were outlaws by the dozen. Gunslingers who thought themselves fast and wanted quick money. But he had to know for sure.

"What was the name on that poster?"

She tilted her head at him. "Name?"

"Of the men after you. The gang."

"The Loust Gang."

Tyler's focus narrowed as he replayed what she'd just said. *The Loust Gang.* He swallowed, but his mouth remained dry. "They were in Cheyenne." And he had hoped they would stay there or go back to South Dakota. Why trail him after all this time?

He was aware of Renee's silence, of the strange expression on her face as he pushed himself vertical. Stumbling to the edge of camp, he darted out into the blackness of the night and welcomed the cold darkness. Muscles in his shoulders bunched and placed an automatic pressure in his head, stabbing behind his eyes.

eighteen

Renee followed Tyler's path out of camp but stopped just inside the circle of firelight. Through the haze of her tears she hadn't been able to make out his expression, but his surprised, "They were in Cheyenne," begged to be explained.

She returned to the fire and cleaned up the mess, rinsing the plates in a pail of water. With nothing left to do, she rolled out her bedding and lay down. She'd so wanted to share with him about Thomas. Her little brother. It made her throat ache to remember. For days she had agonized over how to get home to explain to her father. Until a week ago when she realized returning to her father would only rain down more of his anger on her head. Somehow she had hoped the camptender might never show up, that she could wander the hillsides and work beside Tyler forever. Safe in his silence.

He'd been nudging along her education in sheepherding. Opening her eyes to the colors of the sky and what cloud formations portended. Then there was the sheep and how he would run his hands through their wool to check for bugs or cuts when they'd landed in thorns. He encouraged her to do the same, and she came away disgusted by the natural oils from the sheep's wool that coated her hands. She learned the reason behind some of the lambs not having tails or missing an ear—born in the dead of winter and incurring frostbite.

She'd begun to understand the logic behind herding sheep into the mountains where the air was cooler during the hot summer months. Words hadn't been exchanged much, but what conversations they did share were meaningful learning experiences.

It culminated in her need to understand what Tyler meant when he said he'd learned from the sheep. She thought she might be starting to understand what he meant. Every time he took charge of a small lamb, carrying it on his shoulders back to its mama. Or the times when he guided an animal away from a dangerous patch. Even the patience he had shown when one of the sheep had lain down in a hollow and rolled onto its back. She had wanted to laugh at the flailing animal, but Tyler had been serious about the work of rolling it back to its feet. He stroked along its back and sides for long, patient minutes until the sheep's feet could hold its weight again.

His ways with the animals touched a deeper spot within her. One that ached for the same gentleness she saw him lavish on the sheep. It rolled questions about the man through her mind. She wanted to ask about his past and the wild days he had alluded to, but she never mustered the courage, and with the early mornings, sleep had become a precious commodity.

Renee must have dozed, for the next time she opened her eyes it was to see Tyler across the hot coals of the dying fire.

"Sorry. Didn't mean to wake you."

She elbowed herself to a sitting position. "I was worried about you."

He caught and held her gaze, eyes searching hers, before he looked away. "No need."

"What happened? Why did you leave like that?"

Tyler's right arm rested across his bent knee, the other leg straight out in front of him. He looked, in that moment, weary beyond his years. He scrubbed a hand down his face then raked his fingers through his hair. "Might be best for you to get some sleep."

He was putting her off. "I want to know, Tyler." If she expected more hesitation, she didn't get it.

"I used to run with the Loust Gang."

She gasped. "You were an outlaw?"

"Might be the less you know the better."

Renee weighed what he was implying against her need to understand. This gentle man who cared for sheep as if they were his own precious children had been an outlaw? She searched his face, admitting to herself what had tickled her senses for days now. She was drawn to Tyler Sperry in a way she'd never been drawn to the gangly cowhands on her father's ranch. She'd always felt their respect for her to be nothing more than a thin veneer. They were not men she would count on in times of trouble. More than that, none of them twisted her heart quite like the russet-haired man across from her now. Without putting a name on the emotion she was feeling, Renee crossed the distance that separated them and sat beside Tyler. "I need to know."

❧

Tyler told her then about his mother's struggle to survive raising two restless young boys. When she'd remarried, he'd left home, anxious to experience all the things he knew his mother would frown on.

"I fell into the gang because I wanted quick money. They sent me on odd jobs at first; I guess to test my loyalty to them, or to ensure that my heart was just as black as theirs. We stayed in the hills of South Dakota, robbing miners of their placer gold. It made us money but not much, and the others got bolder. I could tell they weren't satisfied with seed money. Especially Marv."

He glanced at Renee and saw the light of recognition in her eyes. "The leader of the gang," she noted.

"Rand?" he said, testing her.

"The one who kept watch over me." She smiled. "Until you came along."

Lolly, Dirk, Lance. They'd been his friends at one time, until. . . "Marv started planning a big raid. I didn't want to do it. The Homestake was shipping to Cheyenne, and the money promised to be more than we'd ever done before. It was a big risk because Marv had never done something like that before. He sent me and Dirk in to scout the route to Cheyenne and scope the town. Took us about a month. Got to know the people. Pretended we were new hires. Even had a name of a rancher far enough out that no one would question if we said we worked for him." He pulled in an unsteady breath. Raoul Billings was the man's name. Never did meet the real man.

"But. . .something happened."

He jerked a glance her way, amazed at her perception. Him, a man who prided himself on not showing his emotion or feelings. At some point this woman had learned to read him. "I started having doubts about it all—the life, the robbing. Tried not to let on much since Dirk was with me, but then I met Anna."

"Ah. Was she pretty?"

He caught the glint of amused humor in her eyes, relieved, somehow, that she hadn't taken on in a jealous rage. Jealous? Of him? He dismissed the thought. There wasn't anything between them. He exhaled. "Yeah. She was pretty. Good hearted. I thought maybe I'd go straight then. Get a job as a ranch hand and court her."

He shifted his position to relieve the ache in his bent knee. "But it was time to head back to camp and give our report. I don't know what happened then, how Marv found out about Anna. I decided I'd ride on the job and make like I was going to go in then head out of town."

He'd been so mixed up inside. He had wanted nothing more

than to break off before they hit town, but it would have meant a bullet in the back, and his desire to see Anna had squelched the idea. He'd have to play his hand quietly, quickly.

"I don't know if Marv knew I was up to something or not, but I was never left alone. Never got the chance to make an escape." He let his head fall back. The stars shone bright and he reached a hand upward, pretending to grab at them. Embarrassed at his foolishness, he chuckled and shot a glance at Renee.

She laughed, too, her head dipping backward, the glorious spread of her hair falling nearly to the ground. "They're bright tonight. I've often wondered what it would be like to hold one in my hand. Thomas and I used to—"

Her voice broke and Tyler watched her struggle for composure. He knotted his hands together over his upraised knee to keep them still. How he wished he could turn back the hands of time for both of them. He clenched his teeth. Mistakes were often hard to live with, but mistakes brought on by one's own bad choice were gut-deep impossible.

They sat in silence for a long time before she spoke.

"So you went through with the robbery?"

He cleared his throat, the cobwebs of silence making his throat dry and his voice raspy. He cast back over those days, sharing with Renee as much as he could.

Among the gang, he'd felt just like the prisoner he was. Even though none of them acknowledged they were watching his every move, he knew Marv had warned them to keep a close eye on him. He didn't dare try to get a message to Anna through Dirk. Friend or not, Dirk was as much outlaw as the rest.

The day of the proposed robbery broke hot and grew hotter with every hour. Marv ordered him to ride into town with Dirk one final time before they hit the bank at noon.

"It'll give them the feel that you're just one of them. Then, once you've bought some supplies at the store, mount up and leave. We'll meet you on the north end of town and ride in together."

He'd thought it might provide his opportunity to break free. With only Dirk on the trail beside him he could pull out and make a run north or east, to get lost in the Basin or the Big Horns.

Dirk made easy talk along the trail, and Tyler let down his guard. Maybe his friend would let him go. But something deep down told him not to trust the man. As they rode, he noticed Dirk always rode in back and a little off to the side of him. He had told himself he was thinking too much.

If he kept to the trail and went into town, he might see Anna. If he could get a message to her, or to anyone in authority, they might be able to warn the bank before it was too late. He held on to the hope of becoming a hero for the duration of the ride, mulling over and over ways to get a message to someone.

They trotted straight to the store. Tyler tied his horse and followed Dirk inside. Tense moments swelled when the first person he laid eyes on was the town's marshal, a little man with big eyes that seemed outsized in his small head. Outlaws' gossip said the man's appearance wasn't to be underestimated. Sheriff Walt King was pure poison with a gun.

Dirk played it easy with the man, while sweat had formed between Tyler's shoulders and dripped down his back. Walt's demeanor matched Dirk's in ease, the two exchanging words like old friends.

The storekeeper finished up with a woman and leaned over the counter, a kind smile on his face. "Reckon Anna will be glad to see you. You back for a spell?"

"Just in from the ranch for a few provisions." He feared the man would continue to question him about his intentions toward

Anna, but the conversation drifted to talk of ammunition, flour and sugar, bags of beans, and coffee.

"You wanting this delivered?"

"No," he said, too quickly. The storekeeper's eyes narrowed. "Thought it strange Mr. Billings didn't come to order supplies himself."

"We're leaving. Tired of breathing dust and repairing fences."

The floorboard squeaked and Dirk appeared beside him, his manner still easy. "We're hoping to go up and try our hand at gold in the hills. Supplies are cheaper here than in any mining camp."

The storekeeper seemed to relax at that and turned his attention back to filling the order.

That was when events became a blur of activity. Dirk had crossed to the front window of the general store, looked out across the street, and then checked the pocket watch he always carried. But it had been the look he'd given Tyler that brought a wave of fear. That, and the door of the general store opening. . .

Tyler sighed, the telling of the story exhausting him. Renee shifted her weight, and he realized she had moved closer during his talk. He straightened his leg and relaxed back against the rock, feeling the hard poke of the rough surface. The fire had begun to blaze again. Almost as an afterthought, he realized she had thrown more wood onto it.

"Tyler?" she asked, the sound of his name a warm whisper in the night.

He nodded to indicate he was fine. His memories of what happened next remained clear. The events must have taken place in seconds, yet each one seemed to last minutes in his mind.

He massaged his temples, almost feeling the stabbing pain of fear he'd felt when Dirk gave him that smirking glare.

He heaved a sigh and continued to unroll the sequence of

events. "Somehow when I saw Dirk's sneer, I knew I'd been tricked. I moved to the window and stared across at the bank. Saw Marv's horse, and Lance's, and felt certain they were both inside, holding up the bank. I knew then, plans had been made to exclude me because I'd shown myself untrustworthy, and it made me both mad and relieved at the same time."

"What happened?" Renee asked.

"I went for the door, but Dirk drew on me and told everyone to stay right where they were."

Tyler exhaled and closed his eyes. The next memories were the hardest and always the ones that kept him awake at night with the burning shame of what he'd done.

nineteen

Renee recognized that Tyler was in the grips of something powerful. Though she wanted to know what happened next, she stopped pushing. He would tell her in his own time.

"Anna entered the store then. She had no idea what was going on, or that Dirk had a gun on everyone."

Tyler struggled to continue, his Adam's apple bobbing hard. "She saw Dirk first, then the gun, and then her eyes went to me. Dirk, too, stared at me. And then. . ." He blew out his breath, long and slow. "And then he gave me a little grin and I knew. . . ." She watched him struggle to keep his emotions in check and placed her hand along his arm. "Anna ran toward me, her face full of terror, and I saw Dirk level the gun. . . ."

Though Tyler's eyes remained dry, his face appeared haggard. Renee could see the pulsing of his heart in his neck and noticed the wetness in his eyes before he dug his fingers into them to clear the moisture.

In the silence of night, wisps of cool fog seeped toward them. She didn't like fog; it always seemed to rob the day of something. She sat in miserable silence, wishing she could ease the burden of his hurt. His grief mingled with hers in a silent twist, much like the shifting, burgeoning clouds of the rolling fog. She shivered as the fingers of the mist roiled and shifted, swirling around her body and laying a coat of silver across their shoulders.

"Tyler?"

He finally shifted and rose to his feet. Using the long branch, he stoked the fire to a blaze. "Stay close to camp. It will burn off by mid-morning." He cast her a sideways glance. "Be glad we're just on the west side of the mountain now. If we were on the east, it could stay for days."

She couldn't fathom paddling around in fog for days, and even the idea of having to do so made her scalp prickle with fear. "What about the sheep?"

"I'll take Teddy out and we'll make sure they're not straying. The dampness will make them miserable but it'll limit their movement somewhat."

She didn't know why a damp fog would bother a sheep, but she did know she sure hated it. Worry that Tyler might get lost niggled at her mind, but she kept her silence. He'd seen these things before; that much was obvious to her. She had no doubt he knew exactly what to do and when to do it. Still, when he disappeared into the thick fog, her insides squeezed in an agony of fear. With nothing left to do, she lay down on the ground and closed her eyes, replaying the story of his past. Her heart ached for Tyler's pain.

Deep breaths eased her, and she noted, too, a freshness in the air that hadn't been there before, or maybe she hadn't noticed. She likened it to the scent of mountain mahogany, or the air scrubbed clean after a heavy rain, or. . . She fell asleep trying to decide.

❧

Tyler could feel the moisture penetrating the sheeps' wool, weighing it down. The first rays of sun were lightening the sky, though blocked by the mountain peak for now.

Teddy, his nose guiding the way, had bolted off after a few ewes that had strayed out on a narrow trail. Tyler made note of the area, knowing he would have to return when the fog lifted and stack rocks to prevent future wanderings. A subtle lightening of the oppressive air relieved his mind. The fog was moving out, and the dark silver of the mist was brightening.

The familiar work tending the sheep kept his mind occupied and away from the specter of Anna that would have, he knew, stolen sleep from him even if he had tried to rest.

Teddy led the way back to camp, the fog still a heavy presence. Tyler stoked the dying fire and checked the blankets to assure himself Renee hadn't wandered off. He knelt to touch the soft spot his feet found. "Renee?"

In the thickness he heard no rustle of response or soft whimpers and shuffles of someone waking. "Renee?"

He stretched his hand out farther. Empty. And that's when he heard the rush of feet and the half-choked sobs. He angled back toward the fire and bumped hard into something. A choked gasp identified the object.

"Renee?" Her exhale was forced and shuddering, and he placed a hand on her arms, feeling the quivering terror of her breathing. "What is it?"

"A monster."

He chuckled and pulled her closer to the fire where he could finally see the vague outline of her face. "There are no monsters. Was it a bear? A cat?"

The same shuddering cries rocked her shoulders. "Tall. Small head. Long arms."

It was balanced on his tongue to deny it again but he thought better of it. "What were you doing?"

"I—"

Her hesitation told him all he needed to know. "You went to. . .'talk to the neighbors.'"

She gaped up at him then away, smudging a hand across her cheeks.

The fog hid her expression, but if he'd been a betting man he would have bet her face burned as hot as the fire. "You saw your reflection in the fog. It happened to me once before in fog this thick. I'd gone out a few paces from camp and saw this apparition. It was just like you described. Took me a few seconds and a couple of bullets to realize what I was dealing with."

He could almost feel the tension draining from her. Her expression, clearer now through the thinning fog, sported a sheepish grin. Flickering flames licked shadows along the side of her face closest to the fire. His eyes followed the dancing light along the curve of her jaw then down the column of her neck. A powerful longing to draw her close rose within him. With every ounce of willpower, Tyler removed his hand from her arm and took a step back. "I'm going to catch some sleep."

twenty

"What are the black sheep for?" Renee asked later that day.

The sheep had watered and were moving back toward the bedding ground. Tyler and Renee stood atop a ledge that allowed full view of the herd, which made the summer pasture easy to manage. Welford camp, as it was called, had a stream that ran the length of the boundaries, which also eased the need to push the herd from bedding ground to watering sites and grazing places.

"Markers," Tyler replied. "One for every two hundred sheep. If I'm missing a black sheep when I go to count, I can assume I'm missing white sheep and do a search. It might mean predators or that they've strayed off trail."

"It's quite a system."

Tyler nodded, completing a silent count as they stood there. Six black sheep. He stood for a moment, Renee a few feet off, and watched the sheep mill, some lying down as others chewed cud and a few grazed. The littlest of lambs bounced and played. A light breeze blew against his face—cold air, the promise of a cool night, like most of the nights while summering herds.

"Let's hope there's no snow tonight," he said out loud, not realizing he'd spoken his thoughts until Renee replied.

"Should we put up the tent?"

He turned, wondering if she was more worried about him or herself. The last several nights, he'd allowed her to use the tent while he slept under the stars. "Frostbite isn't so bad."

She stared at him for a few seconds then reared back her

head, her hair snaking along her shoulders, her laughter punching the air. God help him, she was beautiful. He looked away until her laughter died. "Tyler?" She tilted her head back in the direction of camp and cocked an eyebrow. "Do I need to gather more wood? I'd hate for you to lose toes to frostbite since I'll be snug in the tent."

Tyler lifted his face to the sky, all desire to tease leaving him. "We'll be good for tonight, but there's a cabin down a ways from camp if you'd like to move in."

She tucked hair behind her ear. "Your cabin?"

"Trapper built it long ago. It comes in handy when bad weather threatens."

He shuffled down the face of the rock, turned, and offered a hand up to Renee to guide her descent from the rough surface. Her touch seemed too warm against his palm, and he let go as soon as she was steady. His heart pounded in his ears, and he forced himself to concentrate on something other than the woman at his side. "I'll show it to you and you can decide. I've got to pick up the traps and set them before night."

She stood in front of him, her eyes sober, and he wondered what she was thinking. Hoping to reassure whatever thoughts of impropriety might be running through her head, he added, "I'll stay outside in the tent."

❧

Renee wondered if Tyler knew what a handsome man he was or if any thought of himself had been trampled beneath what he perceived as his failure with Anna. "Have you tried anything other than herding sheep?"

"No."

"Maybe you could get work with cattle or something."

"Rich Morgan had a job to do and it fell to me." He pivoted away from her and she felt dismissed.

"Do you think they're after you?"

"I don't know, Renee."

She dared to ask the question that had been plaguing her since their conversation. "Are you risking my life by keeping me up here when they might be coming up the mountain as we speak?"

He stopped in his tracks, his back to her. She could see the hard line of his lips. "Take the horse down tomorrow. Find your own way home. I've got a job to do."

Tyler's words bit hard, and for the first time in a long time she felt the claws of shame against her conscience. She hadn't meant it to sound so. . .selfish. Like she was laying the blame for whatever might happen to her at his feet. There was irony in her question, too, when only days earlier she had entertained the idea of never going back to her father.

She opened her mouth to repair the harm she'd done, but his long strides took him swiftly away from her. Renee stood there in silent misery, watching as the sheep lay contentedly among the rocks and patches of grass. Hundreds of them. Content because they knew Tyler would protect them.

A shiver trickled down her spine. She had wanted to believe her father would protect her forever. Her mother's death had shown her that her father simply did not want to be bothered with her. As he'd grown, Thomas had become the one to bridge the gap between father and daughter. She'd resented the silent arrangement at first, imagining Thomas's every reasonable suggestion as the voice of her father. When she'd decided to go off on a cattle drive, Thomas, caught between the warring opinions of father and sister, had come to her.

"You've got to stop this, sis. You're killing him."

She'd known immediately who "him" was and tried her best to tune out her little brother and continue her preparations to ride over to the rival ranch. The rancher's son had taken a shine to her, and though older by ten years, he'd given in to her pleas to ride with them during the drive. "Maybe Pa'll come with me. He can be my protector."

"You know he can't."

"You mean he won't."

"No, Renee, don't you ever listen? He can't. Pa's got his own cattle to round up and send out."

"Well I won't get in his way then."

Thomas had squeezed his eyes shut, his frustration showing in the way he worked his jaw back and forth. "Renee, you're wrong. You are so wrong about Pa. He does love you; he just has a hard time showin' it. Please don't do this. Nathan Potter is not a gentleman and you'll be the only woman. Don't think for a minute that he'll protect you from. . ."

She'd drawn up short at his choice of words, a little stunned to realize the scope of her brother's knowledge of women. "What do you know of such things?"

Thomas had cracked a little smile. "I hear the hands talk all the time."

"They should be more careful."

"Why? You'd protect me from that talk but ride right into a situation that puts yourself at risk?"

His heartfelt plea and pointed question had turned her away from the folly. She had even tried to make amends with her father after Thomas's pleading, trying her hand at cooking and learning to keep house. But other than an occasional, grudging thank you, Pa had never seemed to notice.

Renee stepped into camp, deflated by the memory of her failure to gain her father's affections. By her words and Tyler's reaction, though, she almost couldn't blame him for taking offense.

The camp was empty, though the fire had been stoked and the rifle left behind. Tyler either forgot his promise to show her the cabin or had been so irritated he'd decided against it.

Restless, she moved to the canvas-wrapped haunch of meat

high in the tree, lowered it, and hacked away a nice piece with a huge knife. She could at least make him something to eat. Settling the skillet deep into the hottest part of the coals, she wondered at the wisdom of Tyler leaving so late without the rifle. Even though it was still daylight, the shadows were growing long.

She browned the mutton and added the beans Tyler had left soaking that morning. He had no fresh vegetables and very little flour and sugar left. The low sugar supply had been her fault, and she felt the twinge of guilt for her selfishness. In those first few weeks, he had always offered it to her, never seeming to mind how she mounded it into her coffee while he drank his black. Now she saw how he must have cringed as she dug selfishly into his supply, never once denying herself but claiming the sweetness as if it were her right. As the days had progressed and weeks passed, she had come to understand more and more the preciousness of his supplies and the measured use of each package and sack he allotted himself.

When the mutton stew, such as it was, was bubbling merrily, she moved to the edge of the camp and squinted into the near darkness. Sassy stood picketed to the same spot Tyler had placed her that morning. The horse's presence did nothing to relieve her concern. She eyed the rifle then stared back into the night. If Tyler hurt himself or had a run-in with an animal, she would never be able to rescue him in time. Maybe he'd left the rifle thinking she would feel safer, just in case the gang did trace their path up the mountain and found their campsite.

Renee moved back to the ring of fire. She rubbed her upper arms to ward off the chill, amazed how the warmth of day could fade so absolutely into coldness. Nudging the coffee closer to the fire, she readied a mug. When the brew boiled, she poured the thick, dark liquid and took a cautious sip. Bitter. Very bitter. But it was hot and she was cold. She'd get used to it.

twenty-one

Tyler ran his hand over his hair and down his neck, massaging the knot of tension at the base of his skull. Renee's words mocked him. If the Loust Gang had somehow tracked him and was on its way, he was risking Renee. But there was far more at stake. Only Rich knew Tyler's other secret. The one that could get them all killed.

Tyler chided himself for being foolish enough to think the gang would stay over in the Dakota Black Hills and not come looking for him. If they trekked this far away from their usual home base, there was no reason to delude himself that they were here for anything else except finding him. Renee had been a casualty of their search, nothing more. He should have moved on like he'd planned from the beginning. But Rich had become a good friend and had needed someone to herd in the mountains. The offer to buy into half the sheep had been appealing as well as the promise of seclusion.

After all Rich had done for him, Tyler couldn't let him down now that he had experience with the sheep.

Tyler chuckled dryly, thinking back to the lessons of that first month taking the sheep up the mountain to summer pasture. He'd treated the animals roughly, using the dog more frequently to bunch the woolies tight whenever he got tired of them wandering too far. He'd even tried to force them through dense brush on a narrow trail, angered when they scattered every which way to avoid the tangle of undergrowth.

And he'd reaped guilt for his mistreatment when Rich met him a month later in the summer range at the top of the mountains. The man's expert eye surveyed the herd and his sole comment, "They've lost a lot of weight," filled Tyler with shame and the certainty that Rich knew what he'd been doing. When they rode down to check on the sheep, the animals scattered from Tyler's presence. Again, he felt Rich's knowing eye on him.

"Sheep should feel comforted by your presence, not threatened."

Yet even after that, Rich had been patient. His parting gift had been the Bible and a request to "start with the twenty-third Psalm."

Each word of the book had challenged Tyler's attitude toward the sheep in his care. Nose flies had given him the opportunity to work closely with the animals, applying the ointment that gave them relief. He'd used the time with the animals to put into practice the gentle manner of the shepherd in Psalms.

The small book had taught him something about kindness and mercy and stirred in him a longing for someone to offer the same to him. Rich had, and when Tyler had tried to thank the man, Rich's response had been, "Thank the Lord, son."

Sometimes when Tyler gazed out at the burst of colors in the sunset or witnessed the breathtaking beauty of hidden meadows on the mountain range, he knew there had to be a God. Rich would have agreed with him on the matter. "He waits for us all," would be his response, though Tyler didn't quite know what it all meant. Now, with the worry that Marv might be hunting him, he wondered if God would protect him if he prayed and asked.

It seemed so odd to pray. Weak. Yet Rich wasn't weak and Tyler knew the man prayed, and often. And what about protecting Renee? If the gang lurked in the territory searching for him, he risked her safety by not getting her away as soon as possible. Why should he expect her to stick her neck out for him? Because he'd grown used to having her nearby? Because he enjoyed those moments when he had someone to talk to? And she was beautiful, like Anna. But not like Anna at all.

Teddy returned to his side as Tyler set the last trap. He climbed to the lookout again to gauge the mood of the herd, pleased to see in the waning light that they were restful and calm. He watched the newborn lamb toddle toward its mother. Reprimand bloomed in his mind as he likened the lamb to Renee. His expectations, and the similarity of their willful ways, pushed him to demand too much from her too soon. Just as the lamb must learn and grow, he had to let her. He was not her shepherd, God was.

Tyler lowered his head and drank in the cooling night air. He loved the richness of nighttime in the mountains but something had changed. What once he found soothing now brought a twist of restlessness. Maybe he would tell Rich it was time for him to move on. If God protected him from the gang, he could take the herd back in the fall and travel west, maybe to California. With the decision bright in his mind, Tyler headed toward camp. He hoped Renee would be asleep, that she wouldn't take him up on the idea of leaving. He quickened his pace, anxious to see if the strong-minded woman had already stripped him of provisions and started Sassy down the mountain.

Sassy sent Tyler a nicker of greeting as he drew closer to camp. He scratched the horse's neck. Relief flooded him when he saw Renee's huddled form sitting by the fire, a book spread in her lap, a curtain of dark hair preventing him from seeing her profile. But she was there.

He left the horse and strode up to the fire, holding his hands near the heat, waiting for that moment when she would see him. She didn't move, a sniff the only suggestion of life.

"It's cold out there," he said, trying to open a conversation.

She raised her head then, eyes red, streaks of wetness leaving tracks on her cheeks.

Fear stabbed and he wondered if she was hurt. He scanned her from head to toe and saw nothing amiss. "What happened?"

Renee shook her head and swiped a tendril of hair from her cheek. "I'm sorry."

Whatever he had expected, it wasn't an apology. He opened his mouth to respond.

"You think I'm selfish."

He held his tongue, unsure where she was going with this.

❧

Renee stared down at the book in her lap and scratched Teddy's head as he lay beside her. Through fresh tears she could see the blur of words. "I helped myself to something to read. It got too quiet." She lifted her head and saw his slight nod.

"I'm glad you didn't start out in the dark," he offered.

"It came out all wrong," she blurted. She hesitated and stilled her thoughts to think through what she wanted to say. "I know you wouldn't keep me up here if you thought it was dangerous—"

"Which is why I suggested you leave, because it could get that way if they find me."

"But you also thought I was thinking about myself too much."

He didn't answer but turned his head away from her, his shoulders almost a physical wall. "I can see in you what I myself used to be."

His words slid over her, a promising ointment to the open wound of her guilt. "My foolishness got Thomas killed."

"He might not be dead, Renee." Tyler faced her and removed his hat. "Did you see his body?"

"No."

"If they shot him, they didn't let him get real close before they did it. He might have just got himself scraped by a bullet.

Enough to give him some pain and knock him out. If they had you on their hands, they probably didn't pay attention to what happened to him."

Hope sprang up in her. She pressed her lips together and blinked back tears of relief. Who better to know these things than Tyler? Like it or not, he would understand the inside workings of a gang, their weak points and strengths. She drew in a shaky breath. "What do you know about God?"

Tyler hunkered down. "Know He's here, even now. I see Him everywhere. All the time. In the beauty of the mountains. In the timidness of the sheep, His creation, and what we are to Him if we follow His ways. I didn't see it at first, mind you, but I expect Rich knew I would eventually. You can't help but acknowledge there's a God when you're up here."

She'd seen it, too. It was as if God Himself was reflected in the heights of the Big Horn Mountains. The trees. The grassy patches. Even the wild animals. Fierceness contrasted against wild beauty. Her eyes slid over Tyler. Here was a man who had been fierce and unruly at one time and had grown to become someone different. She wondered if he was aware of the change in himself.

Tyler sat back and stretched his legs out, the position he inevitably took while sitting at the fire. "I'm no preacher." His soft voice crawled across the distance that separated them. "But I know I didn't like who I was. Guess I knew that even when I was an outlaw."

"Did you ever shoot anyone?"

"Never had a need to. Most saw you coming and figured whatever they had on 'em wasn't worth their life."

"They've shot people recently. Lots of people."

He scratched the side of his cheek, the fire flickering red highlights in his tousled brown hair. "They got greedier. More aggressive. With all the patrols out here, it's getting harder to pull a job." He lifted his head. "Your pa must be missing you."

The sudden shift in conversation jarred her less than the idea of her pa missing her. Could he miss her? "Thomas meant everything to him."

Tyler picked up a stick and began breaking it into small pieces. "I think you've convinced yourself of that. It's the burr under your saddle."

Hot denial rose in her throat then sank down to the pit of her stomach like a rock.

"He must have loved your ma pretty powerful."

"Then why doesn't he hate Thomas? She died giving birth to him."

He chuckled. "Don't guess he looks like her. Or walks like her. Can't you see how it could twist a knife in a man's gut when there's a constant reminder of what he's lost?"

Warm wetness rolled down her cheek and landed salty on her lips and tongue. "I just wanted it to be like it was before she died."

Tyler turned his eyes to the darkness beyond. "Death always changes things."

twenty-two

Silence followed his last statement. He drew his attention back to Renee. Tears rolled down her cheeks, and the sight stirred an ache in him to cradle her close. Yet he had no right. No reason. But the desire burned in his chest and took him back to that one time he had held her. She'd been light in his arms. A soft warmth that left him bereft when they parted.

Over the last weeks, she had come to be a part of his routine, an essential part of camp life. He'd never felt so close to someone since Anna. Yet Renee had her own problems to resolve. Someone so young shouldn't be saddled with someone like him. He had nothing to offer, and life on the mountains herding sheep, running from his past, was no life at all.

He exhaled sharply and threw the stick aside, the pieces scattering. He jammed a hand into the ground and pushed to his feet. "I'm going to. . ." He paused. She raised her head to look at him, and something hard lodged in his throat at the vulnerability in her eyes. "Check on Sassy."

She nodded and scrubbed a hand over her face as she leaned forward. Her hair slipped around her shoulder, dark and rich. She reached for a spoon and stirred whatever it was in the pot. As if feeling his stare, she glanced up. Heat rose up his neck at having been caught.

"Tyler?"

He cleared his throat and pulled his hat lower over his eyes. "Yeah?"

"What was that book you wanted me to read?"

The image of the little lamb rose in his mind, transforming

into a mane of dark hair, a pert nose, and. . . His cheeks puffed out on an exhale. He really needed to get a grip.

"Read?" He groped for the context of her question. The book. . . She was asking about the passage he had suggested she read. Maybe the Bible would provide her the same comfort it had given him. He certainly had nothing better to offer. "Psalms. Twenty-three. It's about a shepherd."

She nodded and got to her feet, light as a feather. Pushing aside the flap of the saddlebag, she found the small volume. She shot him a smile and made herself comfortable, using his bedroll as a brace against the rocks at her back. Her hands brushed over the delicate pages, turning them one by one.

Tyler realized she would have no idea where to find Psalms. He crossed to where she sat and crouched, lifting the book from her lap and turning the pages back from Malachi to the worn pages of Psalms. "Here." He pointed.

Her finger grazed the edges of the pages, yellowed by his fingers and the passage of time. "You read these often."

"I do. It's. . .comforting."

She raised her face, her nose inches from his, her gray eyes solemn and pleading. "Will you read it to me?"

He stopped breathing, wondering what her skin would feel like beneath his fingers. Her expression shifted, the corners of her eyes crinkling with amusement. He lowered himself to the ground and pulled the Bible onto his lap. "Guess I could do that."

He forced his mind to ignore the woman next to him and fixate on the image of the little lamb. "'The Lord is my Shepherd,'" he began. The Lord was Renee's Shepherd as well. It was up to him to show her that.

❧

Renee listened to Tyler's voice, the words, and the message. When he finished the chapter, he cleared his throat, hand resting on the open book. She admired his long fingers. There was strength in his hands. Tenderness for the sheep in his care, yet toughness, too, called upon when he had to set traps or take burrs from their wool or give gentle discipline to a straying sheep. "You're a shepherd, what does it mean to you?"

He stared out into the night. She watched his face, set in profile against the firelight. Funny how she couldn't imagine that face twisted into a cruel sneer or his words and actions rough and threatening, in keeping with the reputation of an outlaw.

"I try and supply the sheep with all that they need. I believe God is that way. He might not give us what we want, but He fills our needs, knowing what's best. But just like Punky, we can think we know better sometimes."

She grinned and wondered if he thought her a Punky. The wayward ewe could definitely be a problem, just as she had caused herself a heap of trouble.

Tyler continued, telling her of his scouting trip in the early spring before bringing the sheep into the mountains, when he assessed the places along the trail and removed overgrown shrubs. He often spent time damming a shallow stream to make a deep pool for the sheep to drink from en route to summer pasture, or clearing meadows of poisonous plants. "There's a lot of work that goes into caring for the sheep ahead of time. God's like that. He plans things out, knowing what we're in for and smoothing the way. Sometimes we think it's so hard or the way too tough, but He's there."

When silence fell between them, Renee placed her hand on his arm. She felt him tense, and when their eyes met, she caught the change in his expression. Saw him swallow. "You're a good teacher," she observed.

He acknowledged her comment with a slight nod. His gaze swept over her face, his eyes lingered on her lips, and then he jerked away as if stung by her presence. With a quick movement, he slapped the Bible shut and pushed to his feet. "Best go check on Sassy."

"Yes, Tyler." She smiled up at him, sure now that she'd seen something more than friendship in his eyes, and it gripped her with a desire for something more. "You better go check on the horse."

She watched the vague outline of him as he gave Sassy grain and fiddled with the picket line. Tyler had wanted to kiss her. The thought, at least, had entered his mind; she was sure of it. How was it a former outlaw, a man who lived a wild, criminal life, could shy from her like a newborn lamb? His gaze had held her captive, too, for that long second when she understood the depth of respect and emotion his presence churned in her. The awakening both thrilled and scared her. She'd seen what he had become, his commitment to the sheep, the way he had forcibly redirected his life away from the irresponsible and dishonest tendencies of an outlaw.

Renee closed her eyes and curled into a ball, resting her forehead on her arms. If she tried, she could make him love her. Then, maybe, she'd finally feel safe.

twenty-three

Tyler stroked the horse's flank, and Sassy bent her neck and dug her nose against his side. When he didn't respond to the playful overture, the horse nibbled at his sleeve. But Tyler was in no mood for games. He'd almost kissed Renee. If she'd moved an inch in his direction, he might have, and that would have been disastrous.

Reading to her, he had hoped she might be coming to understand the importance of her actions to those around her. That bad choices often clung like a burr. Tyler sighed. Rich Morgan had probably held many of the same thoughts about him when he'd visited the sheep camp that first month.

He could love her. Maybe he already did love her, but it was too dangerous to love when Marv might be a step away, biding his time. Marv had a powerful motivation, and Renee knew nothing about it. It was better for her to go home. He needed a plan to get her away from here.

Tyler pushed at Sassy's nose, and the horse nudged back. He leaned into Sassy and wished for the solace of the fire and his Bible. Renee's presence seemed more threat than comfort now. Exhaustion punched him in the gut, and he moved, his limbs heavy, toward camp. Renee watched him in silence, yet he felt the weight of her expectation. He picked up a plate and drew in a breath before heading toward the fire and the pot of stew. Ladling some onto his plate, he took his seat a safe distance away and tried to ignore her presence altogether.

His whispered prayer for the food became a desperate plea for help. Spooning in his first bite, he rolled the broth and meat around on his tongue. Not bad. Her cooking had improved over the last week.

"How'd I do?"

The simple question held a note of vulnerability. In answer, he dipped his spoon for another bite. "Real good."

"Did you love Anna?"

He frowned down at his plate, the bowl of his spoon sinking into the broth of the stew. Love Anna? Such a tough subject to talk about, and he was so tired. "Didn't get the chance to love her."

"But you cared for her."

"I did," he conceded, wary, weighing his words. "She was a good woman." *I could have loved her.* If given time and under different circumstances, he would have married her.

He spooned another bite into his mouth, then another, and then decided he'd had enough. Rising, he met Renee as she jumped up to claim his plate.

"I'll take care of these," she assured.

Tyler nodded, grateful to be done for the day.

❧

Renee lay awake for a long time thinking about what he'd read to her from Psalms. She watched as the flames danced and twisted, high and hot, and then lowered as they licked through the supply of wood. She didn't want to think about Tyler or Anna or her father or Thomas.

Her decision to run off and drag Thomas along to look for a gang of outlaws seemed such an immature thing now. In hindsight. Still, she had learned from her mistake. Whether Thomas lived or not, and she wholeheartedly hoped Thomas was safe just as Tyler suggested, she would give more thought to her actions.

Should she have been more responsible? Sure.

Could she change? Of course. Tyler had.

Did she want to change?

She bit her lip hard as tears burned again at the back of her eyes. It wasn't a matter of her wanting to change; it was more a matter of her needing to change. The Bible spoke of change. Bits of memory, chats she'd had with her mother, scratched the surface of her mind. She did her best to capture and bring them into focus, but the memories were dull and she had been young. Perhaps reading the Bible more would show her what her mother had understood.

God? She breathed the word. *All I know is. . .*

She didn't know what to say and felt foolish pretending to talk to something she couldn't see. But Tyler had said He was everywhere. Didn't that mean He was here now? In the dying fire? The night that gripped her in its blackness? *All I know is I need this change. I need You, I think, but I don't know how. Help me understand.*

❧

Morning light stretched its dome of brilliance across the sky. Renee yawned and braced herself up on an elbow. The fire flared hot again, but Tyler was not there. She stumbled from the blankets, taking the time to roll everything into a tight bundle to keep out critters or, she shuddered, snakes.

She moved around the camp, combing tangles from her hair and then twisting it into a knot to keep it out of her face. It didn't look like Tyler had even taken the time to eat breakfast. Taking the bucket to the creek, she bent to draw water. Her hair tumbled down and touched the surface of the water, floating on top for a minute before sinking into a sodden mass. She snapped the strands back over her shoulder and tucked stray strands behind her ear.

Turning, bucket in hand, she saw Sassy moving toward her, Tyler astride, a baby lamb across the saddle. She could tell from the way Tyler moved in the saddle and the stiff expression on his face that something terrible had happened. When he caught sight of her moving toward him, Tyler stopped the horse.

"Cat got into the sheep last night. Killed three ewes and this lamb."

His voice did not betray emotion, only a resignation that told her this type of thing had happened before. "Are you going after it?" she asked.

He shook his head. "No. Probably a young cat being taught to hunt by its mama."

She could see the blood along the lamb's head and the canvas-wrapped package behind the saddle then realized something horrible. "You skinned it?"

"I'll coat the bum lamb to see if the mother will adopt it." Tyler nudged Sassy into motion. He got to camp ahead of her. By the time she reached the perimeter, he was astride the horse and headed back out.

"Can I go with you?"

twenty-four

Tyler debated with himself over his answer. To have her so close. . . He gritted his teeth. He could use the help, and he needed to treat the sheep for scab. Messy work.

"You could treat them for me while I take care of the dead."

His answer was her solemn nod. "I don't mind."

Unable to come up with anything that might discourage her, Tyler turned Sassy sideways, kicked his boot from the stirrup, and offered his hand. She set the bucket of water on a narrow ledge about four feet off the ground, covered it with a towel, and rushed back to him.

His roughened palm scraped against her softer one as he aided her ascent. She settled herself behind him in the saddle, her hands resting along his waist. He took a deep breath of the cool morning air. He had to keep his head. She was just a girl whom he had rescued. A pretty girl. A selfish girl who might have gotten her brother killed. Not his type.

Where the trail narrowed, he slowed Sassy and allowed her to pick her way along at her own pace. Renee's hands gripped his shirt tighter until he feared she might rend the material. "Sassy's a mountain horse. She knows these trails."

"Is that your—" Sassy slipped and cut off what she was saying. When the horse regained its footing he could feel her grip weaken. "Was that your way of offering comfort?"

He grinned at the irony. "I suppose it was."

They rode in silence until Sassy cleared the last of the rocks and carried them into the meadow. The sheep were spread out on rolling hills, while the craggy peak of another mountain showed its balding head. Snow capped the mountain and the sun beat down on the green grass of the long, narrow valley that put the white dots of sheep in contrast.

"It's even more beautiful from here," she whispered.

Tyler didn't respond but led Sassy through the hundreds of sheep toward a craggy spot that backed to thick woods with heavy underbrush. Blood smeared along some of the rocks where he'd found the dead ewes and the lamb. He searched among the stretch of sheep in front of him and listened for the telltale sounds he knew the bum lamb would make, unable to find its mother and denied by other ewes the chance to nurse.

Teddy panted into view and lay down beside Sassy.

"Good boy, Teddy," Renee called to the little dog.

Tyler dismounted and gave Teddy an absentminded scratch as he surveyed the sheep, listening for the orphan lamb's cry.

"What do I need to do?" Renee asked as she slipped to the ground unaided. "You know I'll help."

Thick shame rose and made him clench his teeth. Hadn't he just tried to discount her character? Yet she had helped before. Many times over the last couple of weeks they had worked side by side among the herd. His load caring for the sheep and cooking had been lightened because of her presence. He had a responsibility to at least be fair in his assessment of her abilities. "There's a bum—" He pursed his lips and waited.

"A lazy sheep?"

He hid the grin. "No, a motherless lamb. A bum. He'll be looking for some supper. You'll hear him."

Tyler watched as Renee processed the information he'd just relayed. With a slight nod and a determined tilt of her chin, Renee sank into the herd of sheep. He absorbed the animals' reaction to her presence. Her lithe body bent over the head of one particularly friendly sheep that trailed her a few feet. She spoke to it, though he couldn't hear what she said. A spring lamb tottered over then leaped away when Renee laughed. Her hair spread around her shoulders, and even as he watched, as if she knew his eyes were upon her, she reached up, gathered it into a long tail, and wrapped it into a loose knot.

An ache stabbed through him, and Tyler turned from the scene, glad he hadn't been caught watching her. It would send her the wrong message. As soon as he got through the day, he would get her down off the mountain and back home, away from Marv and the threat of the gang coming for him. But after the damage the cat inflicted on the herd, he needed her help one more day. Tyler flipped open the saddlebag and withdrew a jar of salve. "Renee!"

She looked up, her hair sliding a bit, her face bright with happiness. "He's so cute!" She laughed and pointed to the lamb who nibbled at her knee.

"There's work to do." His gruff tone was not lost on her, and the joy slid from her face.

He held up the jar and pointed. "I need you to smear this on their faces while you're looking for the lamb."

She hurried to him and took the large jar without a word, turning to go when he heard the plaintive wail of the bum. He led Sassy forward as Renee began working over the sheep. A dirty job. Smelly, too, though she didn't complain.

When he found the lamb, working its head from under the protesting underside of a ewe, he gathered the baby close. At least the lamb had received the first few weeks of nutrition from its mama. Working as quickly as he could, Tyler fit the skin of the dead lamb over the live one then began looking for the mother of the dead baby. It took him an hour to locate the right ewe, standing off by herself, engorged and restless. He set the baby down beside her and the lamb immediately scampered to her. Twisting her head, the ewe nudged the baby and smelled along its side. The lamb tucked up underneath the ewe and began nursing as the mother sniffed the baby's backside.

Come on, mama. Tyler cheered the two on as the sniffing and nursing continued. At last the mother stopped and seemed to relax. Tension drained from Tyler's shoulders.

❧

Renee worked until the muscles in her back bunched so hard she could no longer bend over and had to kneel, which made her knees sore. Tyler returned to camp twice to replenish the salve. He brought back cold bacon and pancakes, and she devoured them like a starving dog. Teddy stayed near her, hoping for a scrap and relishing the strip she tossed him.

"We're on the last group," he announced. He smiled down at her, and she saw the exhaustion in every line of his face. His eyes, especially, showed a deep weariness that his grin belied.

"What's so funny?"

"You should see yourself."

Somehow, she didn't quite care what she looked like at that moment. He didn't look much better, and they both smelled faintly of the tar used in the salve.

His smile bled away. "I'm proud of you," he whispered. The simple praise swirled in her head. "You've worked hard." His tone held wonder, as if he was seeing something for the first time, mesmerized by what he witnessed.

Her tongue wouldn't form words. She saw his hand come up and felt the gentle stroke of his finger against her cheek as he swiped a tendril of hair back from her face. His gaze fell to her lips and Renee recognized his struggle. She kept still, her resolve to get him to love her crushed beneath the heel of something else. She already loved him. This man. A fragile love, perhaps, for what did she really know about such things? But it felt right. It felt good and secure. Something she wanted to revel in and cherish, not bend to her will and force upon him—that wouldn't be love anyway, would it?

He withdrew his hand, his gaze surrendering hers. He stepped back and turned to look at the sky, and everything Renee had felt seconds before became vulnerable as doubts snaked their way through her heart.

twenty-five

Tyler had wanted so much to kiss her. To smooth away the splotch of salve clinging to her cheek and enjoy the feel of her soft lips against his. His will had nearly crumbled when he yielded to the desire to graze the hair back from her cheek. Touching her. Drinking in the devotion he saw in her eyes. She had worked so hard, the words of praise had come easily to him. He had kept a close eye on her as he moved among the animals, noting the moment when she had stopped stooping to administer the salve and begun getting down on one knee. He knew all too well the strain of muscles after a long day of working among the sheep.

The difference in her work ethic and the ease with which she accepted the long arduous chores endeared her to him and broke whatever preconceived notion he had of her being a selfish brat. She had grown in the time she'd been with the herd. Just as caring for that first herd had grown and matured him.

"Got somewhere I'd like to show you. Tomorrow, after the sheep are settled, I'll take you there."

"Sure." She nodded and took a step away, her eyes drifting toward the last group of animals.

His eyes followed the line of her silhouette, captured by the wild tousle of her hair and how warm sunlight brought out glints of red in the strands. She'd knotted it over and over through the day. Now, Tyler doffed his hat and yanked at the pigging string tied there. "Here, it'll keep your hair off your face."

An automatic reaction, her hands reached for the strands

loosened by the constant kneeling and stooping. "It has been a trial today."

"It's beautiful." He swallowed, wishing he hadn't said what he thought out loud.

She took the string from him and bent double. She combed through the dark mass then straightened. Gathering it close in one hand, she tied the string around the ponytail. "That's so much better."

"Should have thought of it sooner."

She picked up the jar of salve and moved out into the last group of sheep. To his right, Tyler caught sight of the jacketed lamb, happy in his newfound mother and nursing, his little tail flapping back and forth in joy. Tyler understood completely.

❧

When Tyler didn't move on, Renee risked another glance at him. He made quite the picture among the sea of white sheep. The pasture, dotted with lush patches of grass, and the mountain rising strong and lonely behind Tyler, seemed to echo her opinion of the man himself.

She was grateful to have her hair out of the way and couldn't quite deny the pleasure his comment brought. Whatever Tyler was, he was not a man given to soft words.

Moving among the last of the group, Teddy at her side, Renee lifted her head when she caught a strange humming in the air. She glanced around to see what it might be or where it might be coming from, and that's when she realized it was Tyler. Singing. His voice, rich and buttery soft. Teddy moved off toward Tyler, slow and easy. The sheep, too, were close to Tyler, some of them lying down.

As he worked his way into another verse of "Clementine," Renee let the music flow over her. Even the sheep she tended seemed lulled by the sound of his voice. Many began to lie down, freed from anxiety by the sound and presence of the man they most trusted. Just like the Shepherd in Psalms. The sheep had everything to be content, and what they didn't know they needed was being supplied before they knew of the need. Like the application of the salve. Tyler saw the need before it became a problem, smoothing the way for the timid, helpless creatures.

Tears blurred Renee's vision as she knelt to apply the tar mixture to the head of a ewe. With Tyler's song soft in her ears, she knew she needed salve, too, of a different sort. She bit her lip, chest heaving. *Lord, I've made such a mess. Forgive me.*

She scratched the ewe's face where the wool did not grow then rubbed at the tears that trickled down her face. *Let me be like this sheep.*

Renee continued to apply the salve to the heads of sheep, meditating on their behavior, on the differences in their personalities. Perhaps she was most like Punky and, like Tyler, God would need to be patient with her. But hadn't He already been patient? Even through the disaster of seeking out the Loust Gang, God had brought her here. Now she would return to her father a different person and to Thomas—*God, please let him be alive*—a different sister.

Tyler called out to her on the other side of the group. Pulled out of her reverie, she realized she had subconsciously been hearing a sharper, distressed baaing for some time. Tyler motioned to her. The sheep divided in front of her, alerted by her faster pace. One of the pregnant ewes lay down in the pasture, obviously straining to give birth. Tyler stood off a distance from her and motioned for Renee to come to his side.

"Nice voice."

He ducked his head and jabbed a thumb over his shoulder. "Got something even better. Thought you'd like to see this one, too"

The ewe lay a ways off from the herd, seemingly in great

pain. Renee winced with every stretch of the ewe's neck and plaintive cry. "Is it hurt?"

"It won't be long now," Tyler whispered. "She's given birth before."

As if that explained away the obvious pain the ewe suffered now. Still, Renee couldn't be upset with Tyler; he'd seen the event thousands of times. With each passing minute, the ewe's stress raised. The baby finally made an appearance, but things seemed to stall halfway through. Panicked by the sight of the baby's ears twitching yet still clear of the mother, she turned to Tyler. "Shouldn't you do something?"

He grinned down at her. "She's doing fine. Just watch."

True enough, another few seconds and the ewe jumped up, the rest of the baby slipping to the ground. The baby shook its head. The mother stood for a minute then turned and began to lick her newborn.

"At least she didn't give birth in the middle of a winter storm like she did last time."

Renee couldn't take her eyes off the baby. It wiggled but lay in place as its mama licked over the wet coat.

"She'll lick the baby dry. It helps the lamb not chill."

She didn't know what to say, how to explain the tidal wave of emotions that flooded her at the beautiful picture of mother and child. A picture she hadn't appreciated at the first birth she'd witnessed. It awoke the ache for her own mother and magnified the pain of losing her after Thomas's birth.

"Why don't you stay and keep an eye on them? I'll finish up," Tyler offered.

If she responded, she couldn't remember, but he left her alone to watch the miracle. Every time the baby tried to stand, Renee's heart swelled with pride. When the baby flopped over, a surge of despair tightened her chest. The irony of witnessing this new birth just when she had repented, was not lost on her. It warmed her and she smiled her thanks to God for allowing her to see what He himself had seen when she asked for forgiveness. The wonder of new birth, though, she grimaced, spiritual rebirth wasn't quite so messy. Except when you considered the burden and dirt that sin and her own willfulness had placed on her soul. Tyler rode up on Sassy just as the baby gained its feet and began nursing in earnest.

"Let's get back and get something to eat."

A bubble of satisfaction lifted her on its wings as they traveled to camp. She lay her forehead against Tyler's back, too exhausted to sit up. Every movement of the horse made her eyes heavier with sleep until Sassy began the climb up the sharp hill to camp.

"Got some eggs hidden away for a night such as this."

Eggs. The idea of food didn't even appeal, though she was sure her body had burned through the pancakes and bacon long ago. Tyler touched her leg, and she roused from her drowsy state long enough to make the slide to the ground. Her boot caught in the stirrup, jarring her fully awake. Tyler's hands were there, steadying her as he worked the boot free.

"You're about to collapse," he said.

"Sorry. It just hit me all of the sudden."

"No need to be."

They led Sassy up the steep incline and into camp. Tyler picketed the horse on a new patch of grass while Renee gathered some sticks for the fire. Hot coals still glowed. She knelt to blow on the coals, and pain shot up from her bruised knee. At least she had learned how to build a good fire while being with Tyler. Thomas always teased her about her lack of fire-making ability, grousing every time he had to relight the one in the ancient cookstove because she let it go out.

Renee sat back from the flickering flames, gripped by a longing to see her father and a swell of panic that Thomas might indeed be dead. She closed her eyes, needing to know one way or the other for her own peace of mind.

"Hey."

She opened her eyes to see Tyler in front of her. Concern etched a narrow furrow between his brows. "Hey," she drawled.

He chuckled. "Thought you'd fallen asleep sitting up."

"Just thinking."

"About the lamb? Thomas? Home?"

She gasped. "How did you know?"

He raised his hand and touched her cheek, and she felt the wetness smear against her skin. "Tears were my first clue."

She blinked and swiped at the place his finger had just touched. "I'm just tired."

"Not wanting to go down to the cabin?"

"Maybe tomorrow night."

"What about frostbite?"

She frowned, catching the mischievous twinkle in his eyes. "I see you didn't get your tent put up."

He shrugged. "Maybe tomorrow. I'll throw out another blanket for you."

Unrolling her bundle she made short work of getting comfortable, smothering a yawn with one hand.

"Not hungry?"

"Too tired."

"Then roll in for the night. I'm gonna fill up on an egg and that bacon." He got to his feet. "I'll cook you up a big breakfast in the morning. Speaking of. . ." An insufferable grin split his face. "You're not gonna be wanting to move much in the morning. Everything'll hurt."

twenty-six

Everything did hurt, too. Renee wondered if it was just her imagination, but even her face seemed sore. The sun blasted down from the east. Her muddled mind blinked wide awake as it registered it to be nine o'clock or later.

"Eight thirty, to be exact," she heard Tyler confirm.

When she moved to jerk upright, she groaned and released a long, most unladylike grunt.

"Walking is the best medicine for the soreness."

"Aren't you sore?" She tilted her head his way, noting his casual position. "How long have you been awake?"

"Been up before dawn. Someone had to check on the ewe and the bum," he said, eyes twinkling.

She stretched her arms out one at a time. "And the baby?"

"Right as rain. Need a hand up?"

Renee scowled. "If you can do it, so can I."

"We'll be doing a lot of walking."

"I can't wait," she drawled.

"Good." He swung to his feet in one easy motion, looking not at all like a man suffering from sore muscles. When he towered over her and reached his hand down, she raised hers to meet his.

Humor lurked behind his grin. "I'll take it nice and easy."

And he did, too, raising her just enough to allow her to get her feet underneath. When she stood full height, he gave her a wink.

❧

Tyler had thought about this moment all morning. As

exhausted as he'd been the night before, he'd lain awake watching through the flames as Renee slept. He suspected she hadn't even removed her boots or done the nightly ritual of braiding her hair that he'd observed many times. Maybe women didn't do that if their hair was already pulled back. How would he know?

He smiled at the top of her head as she stamped one foot, then the other, wincing each time, her hand firmly tucked in his. When she worked the stiffness from her legs, it took sheer willpower for him not to pull her close. He satisfied himself with a wink and served up the fresh corn cake he'd made. He handed her the plate. "You work on that while I get you some eggs and a nice slice of mutton."

She ate standing, a smart choice in his mind since getting down would cause even more pain. He lowered the hunk of mutton down from the tree, unwrapped it, and sliced a chunk for their supper as well as some for Renee's breakfast and a piece for Teddy.

Tyler rewrapped the meat and pulled on the rope to raise it high into the thick bough of the evergreen, one of the last firs at this altitude before the balding peak of the mountain cooled too much for growth. He wanted this day with her, to show her the one place he loved most on the mountain. Then they would begin the ride down together. He could return to the mountain in peace to handle whatever the Loust Gang had in store for him. But facing the mountain range alone held no joy for him. Not after tasting life in camp with Renee.

He jerked the pan from the fire, irritated that Renee had wiggled under his skin so easily. He slapped the meat into the skillet, gratified, somehow, by the fierce sizzle and the immediate cloud of smoke that rose up. He stabbed at the hunk with his fork and flung it over, jamming the pan just outside the fire to continue cooking. Stomping back to the pack, he dug deep into a thick canvas cushioned with a blanket. The eggs stayed cool here but they were probably at the end of their freshness, so he might as well cook them.

When he glanced over at Renee, she was licking her fingers. The flash of a smile curving her lips caused him physical pain. He jerked the pan off the heat and took another stab at the mutton. It was almost done. With a quick motion, he cracked the egg into the pan and tilted it so it wouldn't bleed over to the meat. He poked at it a bit and let it bubble.

"Something wrong?" Renee's question took him off guard.

"Be ready soon, just hang tight."

"No. I meant you. Did something happen to make you. . . grouchy?"

He pursed his lips and motioned for her to bring him a plate. Forking the mutton steak onto the plate, he flipped the egg in the skillet with a flick of his wrist.

He could hear the grin in her voice. "You've stomped and slung and slapped ever since fetching that meat."

Had he? "Didn't mean to."

"It's all right. I just wondered if it was something I'd done."

Tyler didn't know how to respond. No. It hadn't been her fault, but neither had he realized that he'd been crashing around camp like a pawing bull. Truth tickled at his brain. He stared at her and tried to imagine being without her. He gritted his teeth and turned away. He was a fool not to have taken her straight down the mountain. He didn't need another day of torturing himself with her presence while reconciling himself to what would soon become the reality of her absence. But he had promised. He slipped the egg from the skillet, set the pan aside, and spun on his heel. "I'm going to gather Sassy. When you're done, come on over and we'll ride."

❧

Renee watched Tyler go. Every bite of the mutton and egg

brought a delicious treat to her tongue as she watched him adjust the cinch of the saddle. Maybe it was the mountain air or perhaps the fact she hadn't eaten in so long, aside from the corn cake, but everything Tyler made tasted good. His behavior, though. . . That posed a puzzle, to be sure.

When she finished, she dabbled some water over the plate. As she swirled the liquid around, she tried to grasp Tyler's change in mood. It didn't make sense. She dried the plate and fork and turned, bouncing right off Tyler's chest. She gasped.

His hands clasped her arms to steady her. "Was just coming to fetch the rifle."

She felt the strength of his fingers dig into her upper arms for the second it took her to regain her balance. "I didn't hear you."

Tyler nodded down at her, his gaze trailing from her hair to her eyes. He dropped his hands and leaned past to pull the gun from where it rested behind the water pail. Opening the chamber, he checked the load.

"We're not hunting anything, are we?"

"Never go anywhere without checking your gun."

She considered that. "I'd rather not go if you're hunting that cat."

Tyler lowered the rifle. "We're hunting, but not animals. This is just for protection."

twenty-seven

Tyler insisted Renee ride while he walked. He enjoyed meandering through the wooded areas, retracing the path they'd taken that last day to summer pasture. As much as he thought he knew the Big Horns, something always surprised him. Teddy usually came along, but he'd left the dog with the herd, lying in the sunshine atop the ledge.

"Aren't you getting tired of walking?" Renee asked about half an hour from camp.

"Was just thinking how much I enjoy exploring. Walking's the best way to do that."

"You should have left Sassy behind."

He'd considered it. Walking would loosen up some of those muscles Renee strained, but he didn't want her to push past the limits of her strength. "Might think differently on the return trip. Uphill," he teased.

"Well, then, stop."

Renee's command took him by surprise, but he pulled on Sassy's bridle and Renee slid to the ground beside him, clinging to the saddle for support a minute longer than usual.

He couldn't help but grin.

"I'll thank you to wipe that smile off your face."

He slapped the ends of the reins against his thigh and laughed, aware of the glint of sunlight on her dark tresses. "Who says I'm smiling?"

She raised up her right leg and shook it, rubbing her hands along the knee.

"Does it feel swollen?"

Turning toward him, she grimaced as she put weight on it. "No, just stiff and sore. I don't think riding was helping it, or anything else for that matter."

Sunbeams streamed down on them, and he debated telling her of his plan to get her home. The words wouldn't come, though, and when Renee raised her face to the sunlight, exposing the creamy column of her throat, he vowed to simply enjoy the day.

"Oh!" she gasped. "It's beautiful."

He followed her gaze to the sky where an eagle dipped down toward the mountain peak. Funny how he'd stopped noticing the birds and stopped hearing the sounds of the mountains, except where they presented the possibility of danger to the herd. One sound in particular he listened for now. He could just make it out. A low roar that seemed more a hum at this distance.

Renee tilted her head. "There's something else. Something strange."

"That's where we're headed." He gave Sassy's bridle a tug and moved forward. Renee matched his strides. They ducked through dense woods, and he held the brush apart for her to lead Sassy through a narrow, choked trail.

On the other side of the natural sound barrier, Renee cocked her head to one side. A smile split her face. "A stream?"

"Something like that, but more." He was having fun with this. More fun that he'd ever thought possible.

Renee frowned and skipped over a fallen log then grimaced as she rubbed her knee. "We're almost there; might as well just tell me."

"Hard for you to be patient, isn't it?"

"I've never liked the surprise side of surprises, but I do love them after I know what they are."

Tyler roared his laughter.

He sobered when Renee slapped Sassy's rump so hard the horse set off at a good clip, burning the reins across his palms and out of his grasp. Stunned by the suddenness of the horse's action, Tyler stared in amazement after the departing animal. Sassy didn't go far before wheeling and gazing at him as if he'd lost his mind.

And it was Renee's turn to laugh. At him. Tyler threw back his head and let loose a piercing whistle. Sassy arched her head, trumpeted a whinny, and trotted back. His hands smarted from the sting of the reins slipping through his hands, but he wouldn't let Renee know that. Let her have her fun.

"I'm sorry," she said, coming to stand beside Sassy, stroking the horse's neck and nose.

"Don't I get an apology?" he asked.

"Sure." She threw a smirk over her shoulder. "Do you want your ears scratched, too?"

Tyler had never seen her quite so lighthearted, and he wondered if telling her of his plans for the next day would fill her with excitement or despair. "We're almost to the place now *if* I can gain your cooperation."

"Don't laugh at me," she warned, though her eyes danced with mischief.

❧

Renee followed Tyler and Sassy, the splash of a nearby stream growing louder, to almost a roaring sound that both puzzled and delighted her. When they went through yet another copse of trees, her breath caught at the sight. Ahead of them, a hundred-foot waterfall crashed down into a pool. Gossamer mist rose where the water struck the surface of the pool. The meadow surrounding, dotted with wildflowers, gave way to more rocky barrenness as it sloped upward toward the mountain peak. It was a beautiful spot. Perfect. Tranquil.

"Great gathering place for all manner of predators," Tyler offered.

"I was just telling myself how perfect it seems. How did you find it?"

"Actually, I brought you here to look for Indian artifacts. Makes sense they'd congregate at places where there was water. You can find arrowheads and pots, scrapers." He shrugged. "It's fun."

"Do you ever use this for sheep?"

"We did until two years ago. Lightning hit a tree, and it burned things up before rain put it out." He lifted his arm to point to the far right of the meadow. A lone, blackened tree stood sentinel to the waterfall. "We figured to give it a few seasons to recover before we brought the sheep back."

Tyler loved these mountains. If they were more to each other, she could imagine that he would share many spots like this. A hawk shrieked overhead and dove down to a thick patch of grass. As the bird lifted into the air, a struggling body could be seen in its claws. Renee marveled at the bird's power and speed, and its ability to perceive its prey from such a distance, then descend and capture with the time it took to exhale. She wanted to lie down in the grass or bathe in the waterfall and feel the water on her head. She wondered if it would bruise her with its force or make her fall over.

She turned to Tyler to ask and caught him staring. His gaze held no apology. Her breath caught at the intensity of his eyes. Hazel, more green than brown. Beautiful eyes, really.

"Are you ready?"

The question hung between them, and she couldn't decide if he was referring to the hunt for artifacts, or something else entirely. He didn't flinch, and the blood hammered hard through her veins.

"The camptender should have been here by now."

Her shoulders tightened. His expression didn't match his words, nor the flat tone, almost devoid of feeling. She opened her mouth to respond.

"Might be time for us to head down the mountain and get you back to your pa."

"I thought you couldn't leave the sheep."

"Wouldn't be the best, but sometimes we don't have a choice. Your pa needs to know you're alive. If Thomas didn't make it. . ."

What Tyler said was true, she knew. Yet why now? She'd resigned herself to having to wait, so why was he suddenly so comfortable leaving the sheep? Granted, they were in summer pasture and no longer moving along the dangerous trails. Too, the camptender was late arriving, something she hadn't much thought about, and supplies were low. Tyler must know he had to go down to restock soon or he'd have to hunt food. His diet would dwindle significantly. And then there was the threat of the gang seeking him out.

"You were right. It's too dangerous to have you here. I knew it then and I know it now."

Her throat tightened and her breath choked. "Tyler—" The flatness of his words, the certainty with which he made the announcement. . . Didn't he feel anything? Had she been mistaken? "Is it that easy for you?"

twenty-eight

Her question seared hot pain of accusation through his chest. In the limpid pools of her eyes, he saw desperation and hurt. If he said yes she would think him a cad and he would be a liar. But saying no opened up emotions that would make things so much harder.

"Things like this are never easy, Renee. But sometimes we have to do what we have to do to protect others."

"And you're just realizing this *now*? You've kept me here all this time. . . ," she sputtered, anger building. "I don't need your protection, Tyler Sperry. Do you hear me?" She folded her arms across her chest, her lower lip trembling. "I can take care of myself."

Both the words and her expression snagged him deep inside. Renee Dover, ever the rebel. You could cover the self-centeredness, but it didn't go away so easily. But what if the basis for that seeming self-centeredness was hurt? Over her father's perceived rejection and the loss of her mother. . . Didn't it then become something like self-preservation? The need to protect oneself from further hurt.

Sassy nickered softly and turned her head. Tyler reached to stroke the animal's side, not bothering to curb his words now. "Just like you did with the gang? I wonder if Thomas would agree."

Her mouth opened then closed tight, lips a thin line. She retreated a step, arms tight across her chest. "What about Anna, Tyler? You think I need that kind of protection? That you can offer it?"

Behind her the waterfall crashed into the pool, its thunder matching the pounding in his temples. From the recesses of his mind he heard Dirk's gun going off. Saw Anna's body jerk with the impact of the lead and sag into his arms, dead before he got her to the floor.

Renee's focus shifted over his shoulder, her lips parting. A second before he turned, he made out the jangle of harness, the creak of wheels. Sassy's whinny made him reach for the rifle as he turned. It slid from the scabbard with ease as he braced himself for whatever threat lurked behind him. "Get on Sassy and ride!" he growled at Renee.

He went to one knee as a wagon jostled into view. His breath came easier when Rich Morgan raised his hand from the driver's seat. Tyler eased his finger on the trigger until he realized a man sat next to Rich. A gun in his hand. Aimed at Rich.

Marv.

He pivoted on his knees and pushed to his feet to see Renee struggling into the saddle as she tried to turn Sassy around. Raising his hand, he slapped the horse's rump just as a bullet rang out, kicking dirt at Sassy's right flank. The horse reared, spilling Renee to the ground. He fell to his knee as he jerked back toward Marv and the oncoming wagon. Others joined the wagon, coming up from behind on horseback, rifles raised. Marv stood up in the wagon and swung to the ground as Rich brought it to a halt.

"Cover him, Lance," Marv ordered, venom in his voice. Lance guided his horse to the side where Rich sat and dug his gun into Rich's side.

Marv's hard eyes never left him. "It's been a long time, Sperry. We have to thank this gentleman for leading us to you. Dirk heard of a sheepherder in the mountains. Sounded a lot like our good friend. It took us awhile, but then this gentleman's ranch hand let us know he was on the way up to see you. Simple, you see?"

Tyler didn't dare take his eyes off the man. Renee slid beside him. "Get behind me," he commanded in a raw whisper, hating it. All the protection he had to offer Renee, stripped from him in seconds.

"Lay that rifle aside now, nice and easy-like, Rand!" Marv barked. The potbellied man rode up to him. "Appears like Sperry has a friend of yours. Think you can manage to keep her from getting away this time?"

Rand's eyes narrowed to points, a laughable tough-guy expression for the little man. "Won't let her get away this time, boss."

So they recognized Renee. He felt her fist his shirt, and a mangled sob shot a dart of hot air against his back where she leaned, trembling, against him. He had no choice. Every man of them held a gun or rifle.

"I like this," Marv crowed with a twisted smile. "Two hostages to make sure you do exactly what we want."

"It's a long way down the mountain, Marv."

The man threw back his head. "Sure it is. We'll let you walk it. The girl can ride with the old man. And then. . ."—Marv nodded—"then, my boy, you can show us where that money is you stole."

❧

Rigid with cold, Renee slumped against Rich Morgan on the driver's seat, grateful for the human contact. It had taken two days to get to this point. Miserable, long days of clawing through narrow paths and staring down the barrel of Rand's gun every time she made a move. When the trail widened, Rand made her ride with him in the bed of the wagon behind Rich and Marv.

When Rand ordered her to sit beside Rich on the driver's

seat instead of the bed of the wagon, she had welcomed the company, even under the circumstances. Whether Rich had given away Tyler or not, she didn't know, but she'd observed the man over the days and nights. His quiet demeanor, the strange twinkle in his eyes on the rare occasion their paths crossed. None of it made sense, and if she seldom saw Rich, she almost never saw Tyler except from a distance.

Marv rode Rand's horse and Rand rode in the bed, his ever-present gun a sharp reminder of the precariousness of the situation. But Rich's solid presence comforted.

It was Tyler she was most concerned for. They kept him walking the whole trip, hands bound with ropes, the ends held by Lance and Dirk, who rode on either side. Every time Tyler fell, he was cruelly jerked to his feet. When they broke for camp, they offered food to her and Rich. Tyler, from what she could see, got very little if anything.

Rich's shoulder felt solid and reassuring beneath her head. She didn't know if they would let them talk but she had to try.

"You making it?" Rich's question caught her by surprise. She waited for the poke of Rand's gun or his terse command for silence, but it didn't come. Emboldened, Renee answered.

"It's cold." Funny how she had so much to say, yet all she could get out were those two words.

"It's the fear talking," Rich offered as he guided the team along the rock path.

They jolted along in silence before she could form another question. "Tyler?"

"He's tough."

She closed her eyes, her throat a burning ache. He didn't look tough. She dared not turn around in hopes of catching a glimpse of him. Rand would surely bark a threat and wave the gun in her face. But the nightly stops showed her how much the walking had worn on Tyler. It pained her to see the slump of his shoulders and the constant rotation of guards who woke him as soon as he nodded off.

Oh how she wanted to believe he was tough enough to endure. She wanted so much to talk to him. Touch him. Tell him. . . She gulped and bit down on the wave of tears.

"You can't imagine my surprise when I saw him up here with a girl. Do you know these men?"

She sniffed and sat up a little, losing herself in the explanation. Her rescue and the subsequent weeks she'd spent with Tyler, it all tumbled out. She told him of Thomas, their search for the gang, and her rescue, all in a whispered voice that Rand either didn't hear or ignored.

"Tate took sick right before he was to leave, which is why I'm here. Didn't know about these varmints following me, though, or their talk with Tate. Blindsided both of us, they did."

She held her breath. His explanation seemed reasonable. She wanted to believe the man hadn't betrayed Tyler. "He told me a lot about you."

She felt the rich rumble of near-silent laughter roll through Rich's chest. "I'm sure he did."

"Good things."

"Tyler tell you about his first month with the sheep?"

Had he?

"Had those sheep so scared of him. They weren't feeding well and were dropping weight. He had a lot of anger in him then."

Anger. Tyler?

"You know about Anna?"

She nodded against his shoulder.

Rich shifted in the seat, and she looked up to see his expression of surprise. "Reckon he must love you, then."

She didn't know how he drew that conclusion from the fact that Tyler had told her about Anna.

"Hurts don't heal easy-like. He was pretty bad off when I found him. Almost dead. . ."

It was her turn to listen. Rich told her of those first days of Tyler's recovery, when Rich didn't know if Tyler would live or die. "When I knew he'd live, I thought he'd die from the hurt and the hatred he carried."

"The sheep," she breathed.

"What's that?" Rich asked above the din of rattles and creaks.

"The sheep. Tyler said the sheep taught him so much. Psalm 23."

Rich's silent laughter vibrated through him again, and for the first time since their capture, Renee smiled. It wasn't hard to see why Tyler held such respect for the man.

They didn't stop until after dark since the trail was broader. When they finally stopped, the blanket of night smothered everything. Rand kept close to her and Rich until Marv and Lolly came out of the dark and motioned for her to move.

"Lolly'll take care of the team tonight." Marv pointed with his gun. "I want the two of you over here." She and Rich followed him to a spot where Dirk and Lance were busy building a fire. Marv motioned them to a spot on the ground and held the gun on them until Lolly returned with rope to bind their wrists in back of them and take over guard duty. The campfire lit the area enough so she could see Dirk and Lance, but there was no sign of Tyler, Marv, or Rand.

By her best estimate, they had another day on the trail. She longed for a glimpse of Tyler. She felt a nudge from Rich the same moment there was a grunt off to their right, and Tyler fell to his knees within the circle of firelight. Marv loomed out of the darkness behind Tyler and stabbed a knee into Tyler's back. Marv's fingers grasped Tyler's hair and pulled, arching him backward. Tyler grunted in pain. Renee's heart slammed in panic. "No!" She struggled to get to her feet but Lolly shoved her down again.

"Stay put," Rich cautioned her.

"I can't—"

"Shut up!" Lolly exploded. He raised his hand in threat.

"Hitting a woman is a good reason to die," Rich growled at the man.

Lolly spit a laugh and lowered his hand. "Coming from a man with his hands tied behind his back, that's a real threat."

Rich kicked out hard and fast. His foot slammed into the back of Lolly's knees and sent him sprawling, the gun flying from his hand.

Marv released Tyler. Unsupported, Tyler slapped hard against the ground. Marv scooped up Lolly's gun, his face slashed with rage. He lifted the gun and brought it down on Lolly's head.

Rich grunted low in his throat. Renee cringed back, shuddering breaths taking tears to the surface. She pressed her eyes into her knees. Afraid of the rage she'd just witnessed, of the harm that Marv threatened upon them all.

"Now listen here, old man," Marv growled. "You think you're so smart. Don't think I won't hesitate to put a bullet through you. Got it?"

Renee strained for Rich's response, not daring to look up or even move.

"Good. Then we understand each other."

His footsteps retreated and she raised her head, afraid Marv would return to torment Tyler who still lay sprawled on the ground.

"Not so smart," she heard Rich whisper. A little grin played at the corners of his mouth when he caught her glance. "He knocked out the man who was guarding us."

She looked back at Tyler, holding her breath as Marv

hovered over his inert figure.

"He'll leave him alone," Rich predicted. "Marv needs him alive."

Renee studied the man, comprehension dawning. "You did that on purpose, didn't you?"

Rich's smile held no humor. "He's like a son to me."

twenty-nine

"Tell me about the money," Renee asked when the camp quieted.

Rich nodded. "He told you about Anna, so you know she was killed by that bullet."

"He never mentioned money."

"I suppose he didn't. It was his insurance, and his revenge for Anna. Marv got hit in the heist, along with Lance, so instead of changing their plans, they went to the same meeting place they'd agreed on when they trusted Tyler. He followed under cover of darkness. Found the money and was hauling it off on Sassy when one of 'em woke up. Tyler took two bullets before Sassy got enough distance between him and the man firing. Must have rode for a couple days like that.

"I was out riding fence when I saw a lone horse at the edge of my property. Sassy never left Tyler even though she was bleeding from her right shoulder. Took some tending to get her back together." He sighed heavily. "Don't know how Tyler got there, but he must have been awake and riding hard for at least a couple days to get up from the Basin." Rich went quiet, and Renee thought he was done talking when he started again.

"Near lost him. If it weren't for Jesse, one of my hands whose daddy'd been a doc, Tyler wouldn't have pulled through."

"The money?"

"Yeah." He chuckled low in his throat. "It was obvious to me right off that the bags tied over the saddle were full of money. Hadn't heard of a robbery, but decided it best to let him tell his story. Hid them in the barn to keep them away from my hands and prevent unwanted questions.

"It took near a month for me to get the whole story from him. The gunshots messed him up and his memory was spotty, but he was messed up on the inside even more. That kind of healing takes time and patience in a man like Tyler."

A man like Tyler. An outlaw, Rich meant. "But he did heal," Renee breathed. "I never would have guessed him capable of doing. . .well, the things that outlaws do."

"That's the beauty of it all."

Rich's words lingered. She thought she understood. It was the change in Tyler, the inside healing to which Rich referred. "What about the money? He stole it from them."

She felt Rich shift next to her. He rolled his shoulders. "His intention was always to give it back to the town."

"Then why hasn't he before now?"

Rich pursed his lips. "You'll have to ask him that."

❧

Sweat poured down Tyler's face. His arms ached. Tendons unused to stretching pulled hard against bone as he forced his hips backward through the circle of his arms. If he could just get his bound wrists in front of him. His shoulders screamed for mercy as he wiggled backward, jaw clenched, his breaths measured lest he gasp too loud and awaken one of the men nearby.

When his hips cleared the circle of his arms, he rested. Beads of sweat burned his eyes and he shrugged the stream away, ignoring the searing pain in his arms. It had to be done. He had to get Renee out of here. Rich, too. They kept Sassy with the other horses during the night and Marv had ridden her a few times, knowing a quality animal when he saw it. Sassy's long-legged gait had appealed to Marv even when they worked together. Now that they were close enough to the end of the trail, it was the perfect time to free Rich and Renee. They could ride Sassy off the mountain and summon help. Tyler had no doubt that Marv would get the location of the money out of him then shoot him. Dying didn't scare him, but if he had to watch another woman die for his mistakes, or even Rich. . .

Lord, please. I can't let this happen. Please don't let it happen.

❧

Renee detected movement beside her. In a heightened state of semi-consciousness, she realized the shifting and sawing sound had been going on for some time. It was still dark. She'd fallen asleep stretched out on the ground. Her arms and shoulders, even her neck, ached from the pressure of having her wrists tied behind her back.

Through the darkness, she saw Rich. He still sat upright, and the sound was coming from him. She bit down hard on saying his name. Noise wouldn't be wise until she knew Marv hadn't sent back a guard. Judging by the snores coming from behind the glowing coals of the campfire, she guessed Dirk and Lance still slept. No sign of Marv or Lolly, or even Rand, and that made her cautious.

A low grunt beside her brought her attention back to Rich. Moonlight was scarce, and they were closer to the tree line than the dying campfire. She squinted into the darkness, able to make out his form but nothing else. She saw him move then scoot closer until his face was near to hers. She leaned in toward him before it dawned on her that his arms were free. "Find Marv, Rand, Lolly. Dirk and Lance at the fire. Move quiet. Get their guns." She felt tugging at her wrists and his heavy fingers working at the knots. "Hands are numb," he apologized. "I'll bring Tyler. Wait by the horses."

thirty

Renee's nerves stretched to the breaking point. She moved with great care through the dark, expecting any minute to step on a stick or roll a rock that would bring one of the gang stabbing a gun into her side. She tried to keep an eye on Rich and the direction he took, but she couldn't see him.

She wished Rich had told her how fast she needed to move, or how long he thought it would take him. She concentrated on finding Marv, Lolly, and Rand first, since Dirk and Lance slept almost in plain sight. Movement at the dying fire caught her eye. She stilled and crouched.

It was Rich. His body passing in front of the glowing embers had been what alerted her. She hoped he found Tyler. That Tyler was able to walk. That Rand or Lolly or Marv weren't guarding him, keeping him awake as they had since capturing him. She bit her lip hard. No time for tears, she forced herself to move and concentrate on her task.

A still, dark form lay on the ground. She leaned over the man. Lolly. If any of them would sleep heavily, he would. With narrowed eyes she tried to make out the form of a gun. Tried to remember what she'd seen him carry over the last few days. A gun, not a rifle, she decided. When her hand touched the coldness of the barrel, a thrill shimmied through her. She pulled air into her lungs through her mouth and eased the weapon away from the still form. With delicate fingers, she picked it up and placed it in her waistband. She crept farther around the perimeter where she found another dark form, this one just outside the light of the fire where Dirk and

Lance lay. She would have to work fast.

Her only assurance as she worked to find the man's gun was the heaviness of his breathing and, if she wasn't mistaken, the smell of alcohol. This man's rifle lay next to him. His arms almost hugged the weapon. Fighting for time, she left him and moved to Dirk and Lance, trying to keep low to the ground. A gun lay on top of its holster, along with a rifle, both in easy reach of Dirk's hands.

She faded into the darkness at the perimeter, searching for a stick. A long, thin, sturdy stick that wouldn't snap under the weight of the holsters. The rifle she could carry. She hurried back to the fire, startled when Dirk mumbled and rolled over, almost on top of the gun.

❧

Tyler saw the movement in the dark. His mind, muddled with lack of sleep, couldn't grasp who it was. He resigned himself to getting caught. His bound hands lay in his lap, arms numb from the effort he'd put them through, wrists chafed raw from the war to break the bond by sheer brawn.

The dark form knelt beside him. "Where's Marv?"

Through the haze of exhaustion, he recognized that voice. Blood flowed freely into his cold, numb hands as the bonds at his wrists were loosened. Rich was free, giving them a chance to escape. *Renee?* He wanted to ask the question but refrained, his mind alive with new hope.

"Come on, son," Rich whispered against his ear. "Go get Sassy and a horse for Renee. Be alert. Marv."

Tyler struggled to his feet. His legs ached with the effort, but he moved. Rich faded away, his warning about Marv heavy in Tyler's mind. That Rich had already assessed all the men and their whereabouts didn't surprise him. Tyler slipped away as quietly as he could, alert for any sign of the one wild card in the deck. He tried to reason out where Marv would have gone.

Marv had always been a restless sleeper. Never one for more than two or three hours before he started prowling. Tyler remembered waking to find him whittling by the fire or working on a bottle of whiskey. He never drank enough to get drunk, but he did drink enough to make him meaner.

Tyler noted the dull glow around the campfire and slipped farther into the darkness. His eyes shifted back to the fire, and he realized something was moving. A slender figure. It could only be one person. On cat feet he inched closer, incredulous as he watched Renee lift a gun and slip it into her waistband. She turned her back on the man and dropped to her knees in the dirt. Tyler could just make out her wielding a stick, digging in the dirt. What was she doing? He inched closer then saw the figure behind her move a little, releasing a gut-ripping snore.

To her credit, she didn't startle. She just stabbed harder at the dirt. What could be so important? He wanted to yell at her to run. He gained the circle of dim light when she glanced up. Her mouth gaped open for a gasp or a scream, he wasn't sure which, but she caught herself and relaxed, recognizing him. He saw the depression in the ground she'd been digging at with the stick. A gun. She was trying to dig out under a gun to pull it free from underneath one of the men. Her progress had taken her about halfway.

The man to her back moved again. Tyler swung forward now, fast, but careful not to kick dust. He lunged for the gun in her waistband just as the man at her back shot upright. Pivoting on the ball of his foot, Tyler brought the butt of the gun down hard and Lance slumped back, unconscious.

❧

Renee scooped the freed gun from the ground. Tyler gave her a shove that propelled her into the darkness. Heart thundering, she shot a look back over her shoulder. Tyler stood there, gun aimed at Dirk. Dirk didn't move, probably in too deep a sleep to have heard the grunt of his comrade as he took Tyler's blow.

When Tyler turned to follow, relief crashed through Renee. She tried to keep herself from running, but anxiousness to be out of the camp, now that her deed was done, pushed her pace. Rich loomed in the darkness. His hands shot up to still her momentum as he slipped Sassy's reins into her palm. He held his hand out for her as she bounded into the saddle.

Tyler broke through. Renee kicked her foot free of the stirrup and held Sassy steady as Tyler mounted behind her. Rich started out on the sturdy paint he'd chosen. They rode as fast as they dared in the darkness, alert for movement behind them. Renee's tension mounted until she realized Rich, of all people, would know these trails best. Tyler, too. She could trust them.

When the sun broke over the horizon, she saw it. Having been on the southwestern side of the mountain in summer pasture, it was the first real sunrise she'd seen for a while. She drank in the colors, warm in the natural embrace of Tyler's arms.

She noted the way Rich kept his eyes to the ground. At times he would stop and let them ride ahead. Renee didn't understand but neither did she ask, afraid to know the answer.

"You might as well try and get some sleep." Tyler's voice sent a shiver through her. She sat up straighter, embarrassed to realize just how much she had slumped against his chest.

"I'm not tired."

His chuckle lit fire in her cheeks. "Couldn't have proved it by me." His arms snuggled against hers as he adjusted the reins from one hand to another. He breathed against her ear. "Rest, Renee."

She sat upright, refusing to give in, wanting to touch and heal the raw, bloody wounds around Tyler's wrists, but the rocking of the horse and the warmth emanating between them lulled her. As she drifted off, she thought she felt a slight pressure against the top of her head. *Must be dreaming.*

thirty-one

They weren't far from Rich's ranch now. Sassy had kept up well with the hurried pace. Tyler frowned. And hadn't the long-legged frame of the horse been part of the reason he'd bought her to begin with? An outlaw needed the fastest horse he could find.

Rich worried him, though. The man knew something Tyler didn't, judging by the way he kept stopping to search for tracks and signs.

They were breaking free of the mountain now. A stream ran near the base. He would let Sassy drink her fill before the flat-out run to Rich's ranch. Once there he could take the money and make the long trip down to Cheyenne. He should have done it a long time ago.

Renee shifted against his chest. She felt so right in his arms, light and beautiful. Her hair tickled his chin, and he breathed in the pure pleasure of knowing that she was safe. He pulled her closer and kissed the top of her head as he had done numerous times.

Rich rode the paint out of the tree line. Though they hadn't spoken since leaving the camp, they were far enough away now to risk it. Besides, the outlaws didn't have any of their weapons to come chasing them down.

"It's Marv," Rich started.

The words stirred Renee to the edge of wakefulness. Tyler tightened his arms to make sure she didn't fall should she forget she was on horseback. But he processed the threat Rich's words implied.

"The ranch?"

Rich nodded. "He's planning a double cross."

"He doesn't know where it is, and neither do any of your hands."

"True, but he has a huge time advantage. After everyone bedded down, he left. Probably four, five hours ago."

"What about the rest? Wouldn't they get suspicious?"

"Nothing they can do about it now anyway. Not without their guns." Rich stroked his chin. "He clubbed Lolly for some minor infraction, which left us without a guard. I'm wondering if that was part of his plan."

"Trying to slow them down. Or us."

"Hoping there are more dead than alive when it's all over."

Renee sat up straight in the saddle. "Who are you talking about?"

Rich answered. "Marv was missing when we escaped."

❧

She should have known. Tyler and Rich said little else until they got to the stream to let the horses rest and drink water. Tyler dropped the reins and dismounted first. "Would you like some help?"

His eyes shone bright, but dark crescents lent credence to his true state. "You need to sleep."

"Sheep and outlaws don't keep strict hours. I'll be fine."

Renee swung her leg over the horse's neck and slid down to the ground. She thought Tyler would step away. But he didn't. When she looked up, his face was so close she felt his breath. He reached out his hand to touch her hair. She felt a tug and realized he was releasing the string that held her hair back.

He pulled a strand around her shoulder and her heart became a wild, twisting thing. She stayed still as he looped a strand around his finger then let it go. His hand climbed to her cheek and his eyes raised to hers. "When we get closer to Rich's ranch, I want you to take Sassy and go. Your father needs you, and you need to know about Thomas."

It was true. She knew it. She needed to end the agony that she was sure, now, plagued her father over her whereabouts. And she would tell him of her part in Thomas's death, and beg his forgiveness. If things didn't work out with her father. . . "I'll come back. Maybe Rich will hire me to work sheep, too."

"Renee." She could see what it cost him to say her name. "Listen to me." His hand fell away, and she witnessed his struggle in the pain of his eyes, the twist of his mouth. "I need you to—"

"To what?"

"You need to find yourself a good man. One who'll tame that wild spirit and take good care of you. Do you understand?"

"I'm coming back."

He chuckled, a dry sound that held no mirth.

"I will, Tyler. I can't stay away forever. I can't find someone else." She reached out to touch him. The beat of his heart, the warmth of his skin solidified her decision. "You're the only one for me."

In the second it took for her words to sink into his mind, she knew he would not touch her. He would not commit himself when he felt himself unworthy or incapable of doing so because of his past. The knowledge freed her, and she rose on her toes to press her lips against his.

❧

Tyler did his best to remain cool to the feel of her hands against his chest. Even as she rose on her toes and he steadied her with his hands, he determined not to give in to the flood of emotion building. He would put her away from him and know he had done what was best for her. He could send her back to what she knew before the Loust Gang. Hope that she would find someone to love her.

Her lips shifted against his and he felt her hands fist the material of his shirt, pulling him closer. And when he finally closed his eyes amid the pressure of her lips and realized what he held in his arms, and the good-bye the kiss symbolized, he could hold back no longer. And he didn't want to.

thirty-two

"We became good friends."

Rich Morgan's chuckle rankled Tyler more than the moment when the man interrupted their kiss to tell Tyler there was something he needed to see. "That's sure how I kiss my friends."

Tyler scowled.

"Look, I can see why you'd be a bear after an old man pulled you away from that beautiful young woman, but we don't have much time."

"We were saying good-bye."

"Uh-huh."

"What's that supposed to mean?"

"It means, son, that you're a goner. Done." Rich Morgan's smile reached from ear to ear. "You talked children yet? I need more help around the ranch. Start 'em young and they'll have all the experience they need by the time they're in their early teens."

Tyler knew the man. Knew his good humor would plow through any bad situation. He also knew there was a solidness to Rich that pulled no punches and took no prisoners. Sure, he'd gotten carried away in the kiss. But it had been good-bye. Renee knew that. He knew it. It was settled.

He snapped a glance over his shoulder to the topic of their conversation. She stood beside Sassy, combing through her hair with her fingers. Watching *him*.

"Friends are a good thing," Rich jibed.

He scowled over at the man. "What did you want me to see?"

"If you think you can be civil, I'll tell you."

Tyler hauled in a breath. "Sorry."

"She's got you in knots whether you want to admit it or not. Don't think I've been around for sixty years to all the sudden come up lame. You love her. Why can't it be that simple?"

"Is this what you brought me out to talk about?"

"Someone needed to. And after seeing that kiss, I thought it might be time. She loves you."

"Did she tell you that, 'cuz she's never mentioned it to me."

"Doesn't have to be words, my boy. Remember, while Marv, Lance, and Dirk had you bound up, me and the little lady were spending some time together. Didn't take long for me to see the way her pendulum swung when it came to you."

Tyler lifted his face to the sky and rubbed the back of his neck. His muscles still held the ache of his bondage. Renee was right. He was exhausted. Troubled, too, by her, by Rich's words, by his reluctance to let her go. "I told her to take Sassy and ride away."

"Why?"

Tyler jerked his hat from his head and shot the man a glance. "I would think it would be obvious."

"Are we talking about Anna now?"

"About all of it. I was an outlaw, Rich. Who's going to believe that I've changed? What's to say I won't swing for the crimes I did? Is that what I give her? She's young—"

"So are you, son."

"She'll find someone else."

"What about you?"

"If I swing it won't matter, and if they do let me go, then I deserve to be alone."

Rich's dark eyes stared hard at him, into his gut, until Tyler felt like the man was reading his soul.

"You wanted to tell me something," Tyler prompted.

"If I die, you get the ranch."

Tyler groped at the bald statement. What it meant. All that Rich was offering him. "If you die?"

"Marv's going to take someone out. Might as well be me. I just wanted you to know that, to give my son something to live on."

He flinched. He knew Rich didn't have family. Had known it since the time he could remember things about the robbery. "Me?"

"You've an honest heart. It's what I saw. You couldn't do that robbery because it went against what was in your heart. I want a man like that working for me. I'd like to think my son would have been like you, had he lived."

Tyler swallowed. *Had he lived. . .* "You won't die."

Rich's sober expression immediately melted. "Good. Then I'd like at least five grandchildren."

Tyler shook his head. "It's my fight, Rich. I've made my decision. I want you to take that paint and get Renee out of here. I'll go in alone."

"You think you're the boss?"

"Rich. . ."

"I'll fork my own broncs, son. If this man wants you, then he's got to go through me first."

Tyler slapped his hat back on his head. "We'll see about that."

❧

Renee's eyes burned with unshed tears. She sniffed and held tighter to the material of Rich's shirt.

"Never thought he could be so stubborn," Rich said.

Renee had to agree. Tyler rode tall in the saddle, his suggestion she ride double with Rich more a command. Rich accepted the idea without a word, though Renee could tell he didn't like it. Whether because he didn't want to ride double with her or something else, she had no way of knowing.

"He wants me to leave before we get to the ranch. Take you away with me," Rich explained. He grinned at her over his shoulder. "Not a bad idea if I was thirty-five years younger."

His good-naturedness warmed the spots of her heart that had so longed for a father's attention. "How can we do that? Marv could kill him."

"Don't worry, little lady; I've got a plan."

Tyler wheeled Sassy when Rich's ranch house came into view. His eyes grazed hers before settling on Rich's. "This is as far as we go," he said.

Renee's chest tightened. Before Rich could bring the paint to a halt, she grasped his shoulders, leaned forward, and swung her leg over the rump of the horse. She stumbled but caught herself.

She held Tyler's attention now. Hard, cold eyes masked the warm gaze of the man she knew and loved. He was preparing himself, putting on his outlaw face. She wanted none of it, not after the kiss they shared. His touch had shown her his heart, and she wasn't going to leave until he knew where she stood on matters.

His eyes raked over her, hard, like diamonds. She touched his leg. "Get down off that horse and tell me good-bye, Tyler Sperry, *then* I'll leave."

thirty-three

Foiled. By a slip of a woman with dark hair and eyes that flashed such an enticing mix of fire and old-fashioned stubbornness. Tyler stabbed a glance at Rich. The man's raised eyebrows emphasized the quirk of his lips. He should have known the older man wasn't going to do a thing to help him out. Renee already had Rich on her side of the argument. At least she hadn't bucked him altogether and demanded to stay.

He could refuse her request and stay put astride Sassy, but her hand on his leg and the memory of their last kiss eroded his resolve to have the thing with Marv done as soon as possible. With Rich and Renee out of harm's way, he would be free to live or die, without threat of watching yet another person he loved die for his transgressions. He met Renee's gaze, knowing the folly of doing such a thing while trying to deny himself. One last kiss. If he lived, he'd hope she would stay away; if he died, it would be his last, perhaps his only, completely happy moment.

Tyler dismounted. He clung to the saddle for a second, warring with himself, until he felt her fingers against his back.

"Tyler?"

He turned and reached for her, wanting to be done with this thing. He was in over his head the moment she curled into him and he felt her lips on his cheek, his nose. He tasted the salt of her tears and followed the path with his lips.

"Don't send me away."

He closed his eyes, breathing deeply of her hair, captured by the scent of her. "Your love will ruin me."

Her hands framed his face. "You'll be stronger for it."

"Not facing Marv."

"What if he kills you?"

Her tears flowed freely now. For him. "Then you'll be strong. You'll find someone else."

"I don't want someone else. I love you, Tyler."

"I can't put you in harm's way. Marv would kill you if he could. Please, Renee. . ."

She rose on her toes and kissed his lips. A quick, light kiss that twisted his insides. She moved as if to pull away. He licked his lips, coldness gripping him. If he never saw her again. . .

He pulled her to him, kissing her like he wished he'd done from the first. When he raised his head, he buried his face in her hair. Her shoulders trembled, and he tightened his embrace. "Renee. . ."

She pulled away, fresh tears darkening her eyes and bleeding twin trails down her cheeks. When her fingers rose to his face, he felt the wetness of his tears being brushed away. He clasped her hand and kissed the palm. He took a step back, closing her fingers around the kiss. "I love you."

He turned his back and dragged himself into the saddle, leaving her standing there, her hand fisted against her cheek. Rich would take care of her now. Without a backward glance, Tyler kicked Sassy into a gallop.

❧

Marv would be careful, Tyler knew. He would make sure he knew the lay of the land and how many ranch hands were working the place before he rode in. Rich's hands lived in a bunkhouse a good distance from the main house. This time of year there were two, and unless Rich had given orders for them to keep watch on the house, their duties would keep them away from the main house.

Marv would have free rein of the place and, Tyler hoped,

would leave the hands alone. If they caught him doing something, Marv would shoot them, no questions asked. Tyler circled behind the main house and decided to ride up on the bunkhouse first. If Jesse and Tate saw him, they wouldn't be overly alarmed and give him away. They were loyal men, both having worked at Rich's Rocking M for years.

Tyler calculated that Marv had made himself comfortable in the main house by now, tearing things apart in his desperate search. His disadvantage would be his greed. If Marv had waited to get the information from Tyler, he would have saved himself time. The man's impatience seemed out of character. That he left the rest of the gang to fend for themselves, too, was unlike the calculating methods Tyler knew Marv to possess and utilize.

Could it be that the heat was becoming too much for the main man of the Loust Gang? Marv was smart, but he was getting older. At fifty-five most men didn't want to be on the run. Age would cause his action and reaction time to slow. And the serenity of a nice, warm fire in a place of his own, far away from threat of capture, might be just the thing Marv sought. He'd probably hoped Tyler would break quickly and when he didn't, Marv had come up with this alternate plan.

The low, flat roof of the bunkhouse came into view. Tyler surveyed the ground for evidence of a horse, or a man on foot. When he finally arrived at the bunkhouse, he found no sign of Tate or Jesse. Their gear indicated their presence, but they were either far out in the fields, shot, working, or tied up somewhere. Satisfied that they would not be victims in a shootout between him and Marv, some of the tension melted from his shoulders.

It took Tyler two hours to make a sweep of the bunkhouse, corral, and other outbuildings before he satisfied himself that the hands were out working and not in danger. They would be returning for supper, and judging by the angle of the sun, Tyler knew he had about four hours to find and deal with Marv.

thirty-four

Supports held stalwart beneath the sagging overhang of Rich's front porch. Tyler studied the roofline then the windows of the ranch house. Smaller than some he'd seen, the place had provided a warm haven for him the fall and winter of his recovery. It had become home to him. Even in the days on summer pasture, he looked forward to returning for the winter months. To sitting with Rich and talking about growing the herd or debating the merits of raising sheep versus cattle.

Tyler cut off the flow of memories. If he didn't pay attention, he would lose his edge. Marv would recognize a moment of weakness and take advantage of it, and it didn't take long for a bullet to kill.

He entered the house with the Navy revolver Renee had lifted from Lolly, clearing the corners, stabbing glances in the places a man could hide. The kitchen was a mess of cooking utensils, pots, and plates scattered across the floor. Cupboard doors hung open, emptied of their contents. Ash and soot from the fireplace settled a black mess all over the floor, showing boot prints leading to the room next door but disappearing as the soot wore off the sole of the shoe. Marv would be the only one with reason enough to tear everything apart. The outlaw must be angrier than a bronc not to have found the money. The damage to the house became more immense as Tyler swept through the back rooms. Floorboards had been pried up in places. Walls sported holes where Marv must have thought a hollow space hid a secret.

Tyler's tension mounted. The last place he wanted to check

was the spot where the money was hidden. If Marv had given up and lay in wait, watching, he would expect that to be the first place Tyler would go.

On stiff legs, Tyler left the ranch house, scanning the area in front of him. When he reached the barn, he hesitated. Something moved inside, scratching along the front wall of the building. Tyler drew air into his lungs and swung the door open just enough to slip inside. His eyes, adjusted to the light outside, rendered him blind in the dim interior. He held the Navy loose but ready. He sank to a crouch as soon as he cleared the door and swung in the direction of the sound. A shot whizzed over his head.

Tyler took aim and fired. Marv grunted and rolled along the ground. Tyler scrambled, ducking behind the half wall of a stall, leveling his other gun on the bale of hay behind which Marv had taken cover.

"You thought they'd kill us all," Tyler taunted the outlaw. "They won't come riding in to save you now, Marv. Not after you crossed them."

Silence greeted his words, but Tyler knew Marv's methods. The man would reload, his mind skipping ahead to escape routes. Always analyzing. Always one step ahead.

"I'm dying, Tyler. Don't matter none to me what you do."

Dying. Such a cold word. Even colder because of the life Marv had chosen for himself. But was it a ploy? A statement meant to distract? Then why was he here? After the money?

"You near ruined us over that girl. Dirk got ya, though, didn't he?"

Bait. Marv was trying to get him angry, distract him enough to shoot wild or do something dumb and make himself a target. But he held the trump card. "I'm the only one who knows where that money is."

"Not the only one, son. Rich told me where to look." Marv's

dry chuckle grated against Tyler's ears. "Men will do most anything when there's a gun pointed at their head."

Acid stirred in Tyler's gut, yet he was hesitant. Rich wouldn't betray him.

"Seems I'm not the only one who knows how to double-cross."

Tyler closed his mind. Marv was playing him. He knew it. Had witnessed the man do it countless times to get his way. Tyler steadied his grip and aimed the gun at the spot where Marv hid. "Are you sweating yet, Marv?"

"I just want to ride out of here, Tyler. You let me go and I won't put a bounty on your head. That money can buy even a dead man some loyalty."

"Not if the rest of the gang catches you first."

Tyler forced himself to think. If Marv had the money, what was he doing in the barn? There were no horses inside and Sassy was back at the bunkhouse. It didn't make sense, so it must be a pack of lies.

"Let me go, Tyler."

"Where's your horse?"

"Behind the barn."

Twisted with indecision, Tyler licked his dry lips. "Throw your guns over here. Both of them. Then you stand up, slow-like. I'll be drawing a bead on you the whole time."

Tyler heard the guns slide across the dirt floor and raised his head enough to confirm. "Now get up and head out the doors."

Marv got to his feet, his eyes cold, haughty. Tyler ignored the man's smirk and motioned with the gun for Marv to precede him. When they emerged, Marv started toward the back of the barn. Tyler wrestled within himself. He'd come so far, protected the money for so long. He couldn't let Marv ride off with it if what he'd said was true. There was only one way to be sure.

"You put your hands against the wall of the barn. Turn

around and I'll cut you down."

When Marv did as he was asked, Tyler sidestepped to the well. Rich had built a shelter over the hole and a platform around it. With his gun on Marv, he used his other hand to reach under the roof. He felt the small latch, grunting as he twisted his arm to feel in the cavity there for the two sacks. Tyler's stomach soured. Empty.

Rich *had* betrayed him.

Marv dived to the side and skidded in the dirt.

Tyler's moment of indecision made him too slow, and his bullet went wild. Marv popped up just outside the barn door. He wrestled with the door. Tyler aimed and fired. The bullet spit dirt beside Marv's hip. Marv slid inside the darkness of the barn. Tyler sprinted to the barn door and stood beside the opening. He couldn't see but neither could Marv, and he knew exactly where Marv was headed. Tyler sprang through the air, arms wide, in the direction of Marv's guns. He caught the man, toppling him to the ground. He grabbed Marv's right hand as they rolled in the dirt. Marv launched a wild punch with his free hand that choked the breath from Tyler.

A strong patch of sunlight swept over the place where they struggled.

"Let him go, Tyler," Rich Morgan's voice rent the air.

Marv took advantage of Tyler's distraction and landed a kick to his kneecap. Marv leveled his gun at Rich just as Tyler struck out and connected with the side of his face. Two guns sounded as one. Marv staggered, clutched at his leg where blood spurted through his now-empty hands. Rich lay still in the barn door.

Tyler lunged for the outlaw, kicking away the gun. Marv dodged him and sprinted for the doorway, out into the open. Tyler panted for air, his lungs cramping, as he gave chase. He skidded around the corner, but Marv already had the horse in a gallop.

Tyler closed his eyes, the reality of Marv leaving with the money a fresh punch to his stomach. With slow steps, he retraced his path and dropped to his knees in the dirt beside Rich. The bullet had caught the man high in the shoulder. He sucked air with every breath, pained over the betrayal. "You double-crossed me!"

Rich's eyes peeled open and a grin split his face. "Is he gone?"

Tyler bunched his fist in Rich's shirt, yanking him to a sitting position. "You double-crossed me!"

Rich grimaced, his hand hot iron around Tyler's wrist. "What are you talking about? I almost got myself killed to help you. Where's Marv?"

"Rode out," he spat. "With the money."

Rich shoved Tyler and pressed a hand to his bloody shoulder. Tyler didn't move to help him. "No he didn't. I've got the money."

Tyler frowned. "He said you told him where it was. I checked. It's gone."

"Like I said, I've got the money." Rich struggled to stand, sending Tyler a scathing look. "If you'll help an old man to his feet, I'll show you."

Tyler was numb. Even as Rich led the way into the ranch house, as his gaze came to rest on Renee's slender form at the cookstove, he felt oddly hollow. She barreled into him and he embraced her absently, as if watching a mirror image of himself making the motion.

"Is he dead?" she asked against his shirt.

"Rode off." His lips felt stiff. "With the money."

Over Renee's shoulder, he watched as Rich wadded a piece of linen and placed it over the wound at his shoulder. "Don't mind me; I'm just bleeding to death." He leaned forward and hefted a sack with his good arm, slapping it on the table, the thud and jingle belying the weight and contents of the bag. "There's one." He bent double again, and when he straightened another bag joined the first. "Told you he didn't get the money. He must have fed you that line hoping you'd get nervous and show him where it was hid."

Tyler gulped, choked by the truth that stared him in the face. He knew Marv's ways. Why had he ever doubted Rich?

Renee filled in the blanks. "Rich circled around the back of the barn and we got the money first thing. He knew Marv would eventually find it or trick you into showing where it was."

"But I got to thinking"—Rich continued, sinking into a chair—"that you might need some help, so we kept an eye out. Waited for hours out back here, watching as Marv made mincemeat of the house. When you came in later then headed for the barn, we were watching."

Tyler pulled Renee closer. "If you hadn't come back I probably would be dead."

"Which is the very reason why I wasn't going to leave you here by yourself." Rich lifted the linen from his shoulder and blanched.

Tyler released Renee and went to the man, straddling a bench. He ripped open the shirt and scanned the wound. "I'll have to get that ball out."

Rich made a face and swayed. "Would like that right well, so long as you can do it with me sitting down."

Tyler didn't bother to tell the man he was already sitting. He took Rich's good arm and got him vertical. "Let's get you in bed; then I'll get to work." He glanced at Renee, already stuffing wood into the cookstove to encourage a fire. "Hot water, as soon as we can get it."

Rich leaned hard on him, and a new worry crawled up Tyler's spine. "I'll send Tate to get the doc."

"I'll be all right. I'm a tough nut to crack."

Tyler guided Rich to the edge of the bed and helped get him settled.

"Upping the ante on you, son."

Tyler's concern burgeoned at the disconnected muttering. "Try to rest."

Rich gripped Tyler's arm. Tyler turned back and caught the distinctive twinkle in Rich's dark eyes. "I'm not daft; I mean it. I'm upping the ante on you."

"What are you talking about?"

"Six instead of five." Rich fell back on the mattress with a deep sigh.

"Six what?"

"Grandchildren. By my reckoning, taking this bullet for you's worth one more."

thirty-five

Tyler's boot hit the bottom step of the ranch house porch when the door swung inward to reveal a healthy, robust Rich Morgan.

"The prodigal has returned!"

"And the lame can walk again!"

Rich's face twisted into a scowl. "Wasn't quite that bad. Tate bugged Doc to stop by again last week, and I told him to stay away or I'd shoot him. I'm not a cast sheep and the buzzards aren't circling me."

Tyler embraced the man, glad to feel the fitness of his frame and see him on his feet. "So Jesse and Tate were good nurses while I was gone."

Rich shouldered past him, dipped water into the coffeepot, threw in some grounds, and put it on to boil. "Not nearly as pretty as Renee, though their cooking might be a mite better."

Tyler slumped into a chair, relieved to have the long trip behind him and to see Rich in good spirits and stronger. "I won't tell her." He longed to ask if Rich had heard from her but didn't. She'd wanted so much to get home after finding out Rich was going to survive. They'd ridden together, Renee on Sassy, he on a bay mare, until reaching territory Renee recognized. Their good-bye had been rushed when one of her father's hands spotted them and rode out to accompany her home. She'd started throwing a thousand questions at the man as they trotted off. But she'd remembered Tyler long enough to gallop back and share a quick kiss and peel off a promise of, "I'll come back" before galloping away with the hand.

The time had come for him to get back down to Cheyenne with the money anyway. Fear of returning to the site of the robbery had left him lame long enough. So he'd kept riding, knowing the long days ahead would be lonely but would also give him time to think. Rich's last words to him offered a measure of comfort. "They give you a hard time, you let me know and I'll get Tate to bring me down stretched out in a wagon to set them straight."

Tyler stretched his legs out under the table. "Jesse got the sheep off the mountain, I see."

"Said Teddy was right where you left him. Guess he'd found his share of rabbits, picking his teeth with their bones when Jesse got there. Sheep hadn't strayed nearly as far as they would have if Teddy hadn't been with them."

Though Rich hadn't come right out and asked, Tyler knew the man waited for his report. "They were glad to have the money."

"Why, sure."

"In the end, they let me go. Said it was a fair trade, if not way too late."

"And Anna?"

Tyler jerked his head toward Rich. "Anna?"

"Did you put her to rest while you were there?"

Riding into Cheyenne again had been a trip back in time. Tyler had visited the store out of necessity, but also a perverse need to face all that his dishonesty had set into motion. He'd asked the sheriff about Anna's parents, but they'd left town and he didn't know where they'd gone.

"Best thing you can do for yourself is move on."

Tyler knew that to be true; the emotions and disgust over what he'd done didn't grip him as hard as they used to. The sheriff had summed it up best as he rode with Tyler to the outskirts of Cheyenne. "You'll always live within the grip of regret, but don't let it rule your life."

"All we have to do is wait for Renee to return." Rich's words tugged Tyler back to the present, the smell of coffee as comforting as the crackle of the fire. Yet he felt unsettled. Something was missing.

Tyler gulped the brew Rich placed in front of him, realizing he had no taste for it at all. The brevity of Renee's good-bye rolled through him, accusing, suggestive in its very brevity. He scooted out of the chair and rose to his feet. "She might meet someone else. It might be for the best anyway." He spun and headed for the door. He'd lose himself in work around the ranch, but he didn't want to hear Rich's voice on the matter. The man retained high hopes for the two of them, and Tyler didn't know if he hated the disappointment of Renee not returning more for Rich or for himself.

❧

Renee wondered if Tyler had returned to the Rocking M or if he was still in Cheyenne. She eschewed the ribbon of color marking the sunset, her gaze stroking the horizon to the northeast. How many times had she regretted the swiftness of her good-bye kiss, sure she would see Tyler within a month or two, the past laid to rest, Thomas alive and well, and her relationship with her father repaired?

How wrong she had been.

"Renee?"

She turned, her father's tall, slender figure a shadow in the doorway. "I'm here."

"It's a beautiful night."

"Yes."

Knot Dover sagged into one of the rockers on the porch. "He's done better since you got back. You know that, don't you? I think the worry over you was hindering his recovery."

She gripped the porch railing tighter, swallowed hard.

"Keller is working with him on getting the strength back into the leg."

Yes, she knew that. Keller, a man her pa had found in town and hired to work with Thomas, had a way with injuries such as the one her brother had sustained. "He should be back East getting an education as a doctor."

"We've talked about it. He's surely more a doctor than most of the ones over in Cheyenne."

From the corral, Sassy spotted her and whinnied. Renee pushed away from the railing and shuffled to the animal, scratching her ears and rubbing her sides. She didn't know her father had followed her until he spoke again. "Time you took her home."

She combed her fingers through Sassy's mane, already slick from the daily attention she gave the horse. Touching Sassy took away the sadness of being away from Tyler. "I can't leave Thomas."

"Sure you can." Knot Dover put his foot up on the lowest rail of the corral gate. "Thomas is a big boy. He'll regain the use of his leg, you watch and see, but there's someone up at that Rocking M, isn't there? Greg said you were with someone the day he found you riding in. Must be the sheep man you talk of so much. He's more to you than a shepherd by my guess."

"I don't think I could be happy knowing Thomas—"

"No." Knot's voice snapped the syllable whip-like then softened. "You're not going to sacrifice your happiness for guilt. Thomas wouldn't want it." He stripped off his hat and swiped his forehead with a kerchief. "It took losing you and Thomas to see that was what I was doing. I was afraid to be near you, to let myself be happy because it seemed like your ma's death required me to be miserable. I won't let you do that." His gray eyes, so much like her own, were dark with determination. "You plan on riding on out tomorrow. You say your good-byes to Thomas, and I'll tell Greg and Dale to go out with you. We'll be needing to get some things together for you that you'll be wanting over there, since I'm guessing you'll be staying." His smile reached his eyes. "Your mama would want that, and this way I'll know how to find you."

thirty-six

Renee crested the hill that overlooked the Rocking M. She glanced back at Greg and Dale and raised her hand to let them know all was well. They turned their horses toward home. She traced their path until they were dots on the horizon, using the time to gather herself, her thoughts. She'd not heard from Tyler since the day they'd said good-bye. She hoped he was home, that all had gone well for him in Cheyenne, and that Rich's recovery was complete.

The chill of winter was beginning to bite. She shivered beneath her heavy coat. Drawing the reins into her hands, she gave Sassy her head. As she neared the ranch house, she thought she saw Rich on the porch. He disappeared inside and another man emerged, a familiar profile her heart recognized instantly. Her tears smeared against her face, chilly paths of ice in the cold air of Sassy's gallop. She slowed the horse to a lope as they approached. Tyler swung down from the porch and hurried to her side, touching her leg, a question in his hazel eyes.

"I came home," she said as she slid from the saddle. Tension ebbed from his face as he gathered her into his embrace. She breathed the smell of him and felt the pressure of his lips against her hair.

"I was afraid—"

She raised her face and touched his lips, his cheek. "You had nothing to fear. Didn't your heart tell you that? Besides, it'll be spring again in a few more months, and I wanted to hear the sheepherder's song."

His arms tightened, and when his lips touched hers, she felt the thrill of his silent promise.

"Well, well. . ."

Renee heard the throaty groan Tyler gave as he broke off the kiss and turned toward Rich. "Can't you leave us alone for two minutes?"

"Sure I can." Rich's smile was unrepentant to Renee's eye. "Just wanting to make sure you're properly chaperoned and all." Rich turned toward the corral. "Tate!" Renee saw a disheveled young man striding from the direction of the barn. "Why don't you hitch up the wagon. We're needing to make a trip into town for a preacher."

Tyler slanted a crooked smile down at her. "I think he just asked you to marry me."

"We'll be back before sunset if you two will hurry," Rich urged. The man turned and headed back inside. "I'll be back in a minute."

Renee rose on tiptoe. "Should I tell *him* yes, or you?"

He stroked the length of her hair, twining a tendril around his finger. She watched as the lock retained the shape and bounced gently against her shoulder. His fingers grazed her jaw, her cheek. She raised her face to meet his kiss. "Tell *me*."

She raised her hands to his shoulders, clasping her hands behind his neck as his lips hovered inches from hers. "Yes," she breathed.

A Letter To Our Readers

Dear Reader:
In order that we might better contribute to your reading enjoyment, we would appreciate your taking a few minutes to respond to the following questions. We welcome your comments and read each form and letter we receive. When completed, please return to the following:

Fiction Editor
Heartsong Presents
PO Box 719
Uhrichsville, Ohio 44683

1. Did you enjoy reading *A Shepherd's Song* by S. Dionne Moore?
   ❑ Very much! I would like to see more books by this author!
   ❑ Moderately. I would have enjoyed it more if
   ____
   ____
   ____

2. Are you a member of **Heartsong Presents**? ❑ Yes ❑ No
   If no, where did you purchase this book? ______________
   ____

3. How would you rate, on a scale from 1 (poor) to 5 (superior), the cover design? ______________

4. On a scale from 1 (poor) to 10 (superior), please rate the following elements.

   ____ Heroine
   ____ Hero
   ____ Setting
   ____ Plot
   ____ Inspirational theme
   ____ Secondary characters

5. These characters were special because? ____________________

____

____

6. How has this book inspired your life? ____________________

____

____

7. What settings would you like to see covered in future **Heartsong Presents** books? ____________________

____

____

8. What are some inspirational themes you would like to see treated in future books? ____________________

____

____

9. Would you be interested in reading other **Heartsong Presents** titles? ❑ Yes ❑ No

10. Please check your age range:

❑ Under 18	❑ 18-24
❑ 25-34	❑ 35-45
❑ 46-55	❑ Over 55

Name ____

Occupation ______________________________________

Address ____

City, State, Zip __________________________________

E-mail ____